THE
REALTOR

An utterly unputdownable psychological
thriller with a shocking twist

SONYA BATEMAN

Originally published as *The Life She Stole*

Revised edition 2024
Joffe Books, London
www.joffebooks.com

First published in Great Britain in 2018 as *The Life She Stole*

This paperback edition was first published
in Great Britain in 2024

Cover art by Nick Castle

ISBN: 978-1-83526-417-1

PROLOGUE

She turns when I call her name. She's surprised and a little confused, and there's a puzzled expression on her face that's attempting to be pleasant as I walk toward her. She's trying to remember how she knows me, or maybe if she knows me.

Well, it *has* been a long time.

"Hello," she says uncertainly when I stop. It's nearly Labor Day and there aren't many people in this part of the park, so she's probably suspicious. And she should be — of me, at least. My purpose here isn't friendly.

I don't say hello back, and she frowns. "Um, I'm sorry, but . . ."

Forcing a sudden smile, I give her my name and hold a hand out. "We went to school together," I say.

"Oh, that's right!" Relief spreads across her face as she shakes my hand. I'm glad she's not a hugger. "Now I remember," she says. "How have you been?"

"Fine," I tell her, "just fine. How about you?"

She launches into a babbling diatribe about her life, her job, how wonderful everything has been since school. I'm not really listening. It hasn't been wonderful for me, not at all, and she doesn't deserve all of this happiness. But that's okay.

1

I'm about to take it all away from her. The only shame is that she'll never know why. She's a means to an end. And that end is coming for someone who *really* deserves it. But things won't be so easy for the woman who stole my life from me.

I have much bigger plans for her.

She's looking at me, and I realize she must've asked me a question. I have no idea what it was. "I'm sorry, what was that last thing?" I say.

"I said, do you hike?" She points at the boots she was lacing when I called out to her. "I'm about to head up to the Sycamore Cliff. The trail's pretty mild, and there's a fantastic view from the top. Did you want to come with me? We can talk about the good old days," she says with a grin.

I look from her to the nearby mountain towering above, imagining the rocky cliffs and the sheer drop from the top. Imagining how she'll look when I push her off, the shock and dismay on her pretty face as she plummets to her death. And I smile.

"I'd love to," I say. "Let's go."

CHAPTER 1

It's the first day of kindergarten, and my daughter is so excited I'm afraid she might pop like a soap bubble.

Alyssa practically vibrates in her booster seat as we pull into the parking lot of Wolfsbrook Elementary. She's four and small for her age, turning five in October, but she's not underdeveloped or stunted. Just naturally tiny. My little dark-haired, green-eyed pixie, with her button nose and her smile that lights up a room. She charms everyone she meets, so I'm not worried that she'll have trouble adjusting to full-time school.

I'm the one who's having adjustment issues. Even though I promised myself I wouldn't cry, my eyes sting a little as I pounce on an empty parking space and turn off the car. This is it. My baby is taking her first step into the long tides of growing up.

I catch myself envisioning what a wreck I'll be when she graduates high school and force the thought away. There's still plenty of time before that.

And I have other things to cry about today.

"We're here!" Alyssa calls out as she unbuckles her seat belt. "Can I open the door by myself, Mommy?"

I flash a smile over the seat at her. "Yes, but wait until I get to your side of the car, okay?" I say. "There's a lot of traffic here right now."

"Okay. I'll wait."

I disengage the safety locks, grab my purse and get out. I've drilled traffic safety into her from basically the day she took her first steps, because she's so tiny. If she were in the path of a car, any car, the driver would never see her. The thought of it gives me nightmares.

I'm amazed at the amount of activity here this morning. When Alyssa and I visited the school last week to see her classroom and meet Mrs. Jocasta, her teacher, there were only a handful of cars in the lot and none in the curved drive that runs in front of the building. Now the drive is packed with bumblebee-yellow buses, and the parking lot is crammed full, with spillover onto the shoulder of the main road and the side streets. The first day of school is a madhouse of kids catching up with friends and showing off new clothes and gear, while parents and school staff race to corral the excitement and direct the flow inside.

Of course, it would've been the same way when I went to school here, but I never noticed the traffic or the adults. I was just another child in the throng.

So was Rosalie Phillips.

As I look toward the entrance and the bustle of little people swarming the sidewalks, I actually *see* her for just an instant as she was in second grade — her dark hair in pigtails, the gap between her front teeth that by high school would be corrected through two embarrassing middle-school years of braces, the sundresses she wore so often, even in winter over a turtleneck and thick tights. We hadn't been best friends or anything, but she was in my grade and I knew her.

"Mommy, can I open the door yet?"

Alyssa's voice, muffled inside the car, startles me. The vision of little Rosalie fades as I hurry around the back and stand just behind her door. "Okay, baby. Come on out," I say.

She pops the handle on the first try and scrambles out, tugging her brand new My Little Pony backpack along with her. Then she shuts the door, threads one arm through the backpack strap, and struggles to get the other one. Soon she's turning in circles like a dog chasing its tail, trying to catch the elusive second strap with her free hand.

I hold back a laugh. "Want some help with that, munchkin?"

"I can do it," she says with the supreme confidence of the very young. Three more tries, and she finally manages to slip her arm behind the strap, beaming up at me. "See?"

"Yes, you can," I say to Little Miss Independent.

I take her hand, and we start across the parking lot toward the slight, grassy rise that leads to the main drive. A thirty-something woman in a safety-orange vest, holding a red stop sign on a stick, stands on the opposite side of the crosswalk in front of the line of buses. She crosses when she sees us coming and smiles broadly at Alyssa.

My daughter returns the smile with a thousand extra watts. "Hi! I'm Alyssa Dawn Bauman," she says. "I go to this school now, like my mommy did."

I resist the urge to remind her not to give strangers her full name. People in uniform are the exception, and this crossing guard has a badge.

"Well, hello there, Alyssa Dawn Bauman," the crossing guard says. "It's nice to meet you. I'm Ms. Fischer."

"Hi, Ms. Fischer!"

The crossing guard laughs, then grabs the silver whistle hanging from the cord around her neck and holds the stop sign out toward the traffic. As we cross behind her, Alyssa tugs my hand and points at something with her free hand. "Who's that, Mommy?" she whispers loudly. "Is she famous?"

I follow her gesture to the waist-high, wrought iron fence that runs from the back wall of the school building across the yard to the end of the main drive. There's a lone woman standing behind the fence — late twenties like me, rail-thin and dressed in a white silk something that looks like a robe, with strappy black heels and a huge pair of dark sunglasses over full lips painted blood-red. Loosely curled, platinum-blond hair tumbles past her shoulders, and a cigarette smolders in one slender hand.

She's just standing there, staring at the children on the sidewalk.

Something about her sets off a low-grade alarm in my gut. Maybe it's because she's wearing a bathrobe and heels in public — odd, to say the least — or because she's hanging around an elementary school without a child, smoking a cigarette, and she obviously doesn't work here. This picture doesn't add up.

"I don't think she's famous, honey," I say as I hurry Alyssa along. "Come on, let's go find your teacher."

Once we get inside the building, my faint feeling of unease dissolves. Alyssa remembers the way to her classroom faster than I do, and she tugs me excitedly down one hallway after another without pause until we reach the kindergarten wing, where the teachers stand outside their doors to greet the newest students.

Wolfsbrook, New Hampshire, is a good-sized suburb full of middle- and upper-class money, and the elementary school has four kindergarten rooms, each staffed with a teacher and at least one assistant. This keeps the class sizes under twenty students. And Mrs. Jocasta apparently remembers each one of hers, because she greets my daughter by name when we reach the door.

"Good morning, Alyssa," the teacher says brightly. She's a pretty woman in her early thirties, with thick strawberry-blond hair and a very white smile. "Can you find your name on your cubby and hang up your backpack? If you need help, just ask Mrs. Field."

"Good morning, Mrs. Jocasta. I can read my name," Alyssa says with a proud smile. For a minute I think she'll dash into the room without a backwards glance, and my heart will break a little, but she turns and throws her arms around my waist. "Bye, Mommy," she says.

I squeeze her back and lean down for a kiss. "Bye, munchkin," I say, my voice just a little bit unsteady. "I'll be here when you're done, and you can tell me all about your first day of school. Remember, don't go outside without me, okay?"

"I won't. Love you! Bye!" She breaks off, then turns and waves from the doorway.

I wave back. "I love you too!"

With that, she vanishes into the cloud of giggles and chatters and brightly colored everything that is kindergarten.

"I think Alyssa will be just fine, Mrs. Bauman."

I jump a little when Mrs. Jocasta speaks. I'd almost forgotten she was there, but she's regarding me with a patient smile — probably the same one she wears for every parent leaving their precious darlings in a classroom for the first time. "It's Ms. Bauman. Call me Celine, actually," I say. "And thank you. I know she will be."

Mrs. Jocasta doesn't react to my lack of marital status or ask questions about Alyssa's father, and I'm grateful for that. He's a long, complicated story. She just gives me another smile and says, "Celine, then. I look forward to having her in my class."

I make an appropriate response, something along the lines of thank you and goodbye and see you after school. My eyes are misting up, and I have to walk away before I give in to the urge to grab my daughter and take her home, declare that she's not ready to start school yet when *I'm* the one who isn't ready for this.

Once I get outside and away from the crowds, I'm more or less okay. I notice that the creepy movie-star woman is gone, or at least not at the fence anymore, but there's something else on my mind now — where I have to go next.

Most of the time I'm grateful that my job is so flexible. I don't have to be in the office much, and making the adjustments to bring Alyssa to school and pick her up hasn't been a problem. But right now I almost wish I had a more traditional job, because I might've used it as an excuse not to go to the funeral. This isn't going to be easy.

I didn't know her well, but I knew her enough. And now, Rosalie Phillips is never going to see her thirtieth birthday.

CHAPTER 2

It's 9:30 when I arrive at the Baker-Lindstrom Funeral Home, the preferred choice of burial services among the wealthier and older families of Wolfsbrook. The rest of us usually opted for the less-stuffy atmosphere of Morris and Sons across town, where the few funerals I'd attended in my life had been held. All except one, but I try not to think about that funeral. The one I almost didn't make it through.

This place feels more like a golf course than a funeral home, complete with well-tended grounds and gardens, and a parking lot that's smooth as black glass. Like the elementary school lot, this one is nearly full. But it's not only cars gathered outside. There are knots of people in dark, formal dress huddled here and there, holding subdued conversations under the bright September sun.

Rosalie's family has opted for a compressed mourning period. One day only, calling hours from nine to eleven, graveside funeral at 11:30. On the surface it looks almost callous, as if they want to get this over with and move on with their lives. But I suspect in this case it's overwhelming grief and shock, and the need to spend as little time as possible being actively reminded of their tragedy. Not just because she was only twenty-eight, but because of the way she died.

Four days ago, Rosalie Phillips jumped off the top of a cliff at Juniper State Park and Reservoir, deliberately swan-diving to the end of her life.

No one knows why she did it. She was happily engaged, at the start of a promising career, and in the middle of planning her parents' thirtieth wedding anniversary. She was healthy and fit, loved the outdoors, and had spent a lot of weekends hiking that park since high school. But even with those slim-to-none chances of an accident, it was clearly a suicide. Because she'd left a note.

Chills invade my blood as I park my gray Montego next to a bright yellow pickup, and I grip the steering wheel hard as they subside. My own shock at hearing about Rosalie has kept me insulated from deeper emotions, but now I'm starting to feel weak and small. Almost terrified. A girl I knew is lying dead in that building, less than a hundred feet away from me. And she *chose* to be dead.

That's when I realize it's not just horror and sadness I'm feeling. Most of this brick of emotion that's lodged in my throat and trying to choke me is guilt. But I have to get through this somehow.

I have to remember that unlike the one before this, Rosalie's death isn't my fault.

I manage to pull myself together and climb out of the car, scanning the parking lot for a familiar red Fiat. Just as I spot the vehicle three rows away and head toward it, the front door opens and Jill Mazer emerges, wearing a black short-sleeved pantsuit with her usually scattered brown hair tamed into a neat bun.

I'm so relieved to see her that I almost manage a smile. She hugs me, and the tears I'm trying to hold back come closer than ever to falling. "Thank you so much for coming," I say. "You didn't have to, you know."

"Of course I did. What are friends for?" Jill squeezes my hand briefly and nods toward the funeral home. "Do you want to go right in, or . . . ?"

"In a minute," I say on a shaky breath. I really am grateful that she's here. She grew up in the city — Oslow, where most of us went to the state university after high school — and she'd only met Rosalie once or twice. But Jill and I clicked instantly during the first semester of sophomore year at college, while we were in English Comp II together, and we'd been best friends ever since. She'd even moved to Wolfsbrook after graduation, and she lived just a few blocks from me and Alyssa.

With my daughter's father out of the picture, she'd been a real godsend.

Jill gives me a sympathetic smile. "You look awful," she says. "Are you sure you want to do this? Maybe we should go somewhere and get coffee instead."

"No, it's fine. I'll be fine." I sniffle once, making a lie out of the statement, but I'm still determined to hold it together. At least long enough to find Rosalie's parents and offer my condolences — for all the good it'll do them. "God, I hate funerals," I say.

Jill nods solemnly. "Me too. Remember that girl Joan, back in college?"

Oh, God. Hearing that name is like a punch in the face. I close my eyes and hope I don't look as guilty as I feel — which is just as strong as the day of her funeral, when I sat in the back row trying to avoid everyone's gazes, convinced I might as well be wearing a neon sign that flashed I KILLED HER to the world.

I never told Jill, or anyone else, what happened. At first I was too scared, and then . . . well, I just couldn't. Some secrets only get bigger and stronger with time, until they're so big that they're sure to kill you on the way out. And one way or another, they'll follow you to the grave.

"Yes, I remember," I finally say in a strained tone that sounds mostly like sorrow. "Were you there, too?" I couldn't recall seeing Jill that day, but we hadn't met each other yet. The thing with Joan happened toward the end of freshman year.

Jill shakes her head. "I didn't really know her that well," she says. "I went to the calling hours the night before, because everybody was going, but I had an Intro to Law exam the morning of the funeral. Believe me, the calling hours were sad enough."

It's my turn to nod numbly. I force my thoughts away from the past and square my shoulders. "Okay. Let's get this over with," I say.

We cross the rest of the parking lot together and step onto the long sidewalk leading to the funeral home entrance. Rows of small brass urns with bright flowers growing out of them line both sides of the marble walkway, with twin expanses of emerald-green grass rolling out past the flowers to the tree-lined borders of the property. More knots of people dot the grass and the various shaded benches as they wait anxiously for the main event to begin.

For some reason, the whole scene makes me think about how much funerals and weddings have in common. A large gathering of relatives and friends at an elegant venue, an air of solemn anticipation, lots of people crying, a traditional ceremony followed by a second gathering for food and reminiscing. But they're at opposite ends of the spectrum — one is for beginnings, another for endings.

The thought of the wedding Rosalie will never have tightens my throat.

As Jill and I head up the sidewalk, a trio of young women emerge from the open doors of the funeral home and head toward us. They're all high school classmates, and I recognize them as some of Rosalie's good friends. In fact, the one in the middle, Missy Wilson, might've been her best friend, or close to it.

Missy was also prone to histrionics, the drama queen of Wolfsbrook High. And it looks like she hasn't lost any of her flair for the dramatic. She wails at the top of her lungs as she wobbles on three-inch spiked heels, leaning on the other two for support as tears stream from her reddened eyes.

I feel bad for remembering what she was like and ascribing it to her now. Her grief is probably genuine. But she's also Making A Scene, and I can't help thinking that she loves the attention despite her actual sorrow for her friend.

Missy spots me and homes in like a guided missile, her face crumpling all over again as she teeters toward me and flings her arms out. "Oh, Celine!" she cries. "I'm so glad you came. Isn't it just *awful*?"

Before I can stop it, I'm folded into a cloud of slender limbs and expensive perfume, and I have to hug her back.

"Hi, Missy," I finally say when I manage to extricate myself. The other two, Liza and Georgette, are hanging back and wringing their hands like chorus girls in a tragic stage play. "I'm so sorry for your loss."

It's not exactly her loss, I think with a twinge of spite, and hate myself for it. I'm not supposed to think ill of others — if nothing else, my mother has drilled that into me. But I can't help it. She's so over-the-top, and some of it is definitely calculated. She'll probably milk sympathy out of Rosalie's death for years.

"God. I still can't believe it," Missy says, producing a lace handkerchief from somewhere to dab at her eyes. "Did you know that she asked her to go with me that day? She really did," she adds with the air of someone who's already told this story dozens of times and embellished it with every telling. "But I had a hair appointment with Rafael, and I'd made it months ago. It's just so hard to book him, you know? Oh, I should have cancelled my appointment anyway!"

She dissolves into loud wailing again, and both Liza and Georgette surge forward to brace her against collapse.

"I'm so sorry," I repeat, careful not to say *that's awful* or anything else she'd view as a condemnation of her character. Honestly, I didn't believe Missy Wilson had set foot in Juniper Park — or any large outdoor space, for that matter — in her entire life, but who knows? Maybe Rosalie really did ask her to come out. Not that she'd ever have agreed to do it, regardless of any fancy hair appointments.

As Missy struggles to pull herself together, I look around the grounds, hoping Rosalie's parents might come out for air so I can give my condolences and leave. I dread the idea of entering that building. I'm not surprised when I don't spot them . . . but I'm struck breathless when I notice a different familiar figure standing by one of the outdoor cigarette stations.

It's the woman I saw at the elementary school this morning. Still wearing dark glasses and red lipstick, but with a black cocktail dress and patent leather flats instead of the white robe and strappy heels.

She seems to be staring straight at me.

Jill nudges me. "What's wrong?" she says under her breath. "You look like you've seen a ghost."

I start to reply, but then I realize Missy is talking again. And the few words I catch from her make my heart stop and drive all thoughts of the mystery woman from my head: ". . . he woke up last night."

"What?" I whisper, gaping at her. "What did you say?"

The look she gives me is part miserable, part insulted. She still isn't happy unless people are hanging on her every word, just like high school. "I said, if only she'd held on for three more days, she could've told Brad how she felt. He woke up last night." Missy narrows her eyes slightly. "Didn't you know that? I thought you and Brad were an item for a while."

Oh, God, I can't breathe. Brad is *awake*?

"She just loved him so much," Missy simpers through the dizzying rush in my head. "I mean, nobody ever knew. She was only with him for a week in college, and even *I* thought she'd gotten over him forever ago. She was marrying Reid, after all. But she left that note, saying how she couldn't live without Brad, and it's all so . . . Celine? Are you okay?"

"Fine. I'm fine," I croak desperately. "I just . . . need to sit down."

Jill puts an arm around me and starts dragging me toward a shaded bench, leaving Missy and her chorus girls standing there, looking hurt and confused. I try to murmur something about catching up with them later, but I don't think what leaves my mouth makes any sense. I can't think straight. Something inside me is shattering to pieces, and I'm not sure it'll ever be fixed again.

Brad Dowling has been in a coma for just over five years. No one ever thought he'd wake up, least of all me. In fact, I'd built my life around knowing he was never coming back. I didn't have a choice in the matter. Hoping for a miracle would've destroyed me. But now that the miracle has happened, I have no idea what to do.

One way or another, my carefully constructed, mostly stable little life is about to fall apart.

CHAPTER 3

You can't tell him, Celine. You just can't.

Jill is right — at least for now. That's what she said to me once I managed to catch my breath and purge the flood of memories I'd kept locked away for so long. If Brad really is awake after all this time, he'll have a lot to deal with. There's also the fact that his parents are sure to be there with him, and they despise me. Blame me for the accident. They might not let me see him.

And honestly, there's a good chance Missy is full of shit, and he's not really awake.

Whether or not it's true, I couldn't face Rosalie's parents or the rest of the funeral. Jill and I had gone for coffee and then headed our separate ways to work — her to the legal office of Lindstrom, Gores and Carolin, and me to Hughes Real Estate. I hadn't stayed long at the office, though. I had a showing this afternoon, and then I'd cleared the rest of the day to pick up Alyssa and celebrate her first day of school.

Now I'm parked in the driveway of my problem-child listing: a five-bedroom, three-bath Victorian with all the bells and whistles that's been on the market for over two years. The sellers, Mr. and Mrs. Quintaine, have been the most challenging clients I've ever worked with. They put the house up a week before they moved to Florida, demanding a selling price of four hundred thousand and not a penny less. Since then they've turned down every purchase offer like clockwork, up to and including one for three hundred and ninety-five thousand.

Sometimes I wonder why I bother with this one, or why the Quintaines haven't gone looking for a new agent who didn't beg them to consider knocking a lousy five grand off the asking price. But I suppose it's because of the twelve-thousand-dollar payday I'll get if I ever manage to sell this place.

Promptly at noon, a car slows and pulls into the driveway behind me — an electric blue two-door Lexus sports model with tinted windows, gleaming and showroom-new. At least it looks like the buyer can afford this place. I only know her name, Hannah Byers, and that she's new to Wolfsbrook. She called me directly yesterday morning to set up the appointment, saying she'd found my name and number online as the listing agent.

I put on my welcoming smile and get out of the car, briefcase in hand. But when the Lexus door opens and Hannah Byers emerges, the smile freezes into a shocked grimace on my face.

It's her. The woman I saw at the school this morning, and again at the funeral. She's still in the little black dress and pumps, sunglasses in place, with a red Hermès purse that matches her red lips curved into an uncertain smile.

"Hello," she calls as she closes the car door and glides toward me. "Are you Celine Bauman?"

For a moment I'm not sure I'll be able to answer. The vague unease I felt when I first saw her returns, stronger this time, and my hind brain tries to tell me that she's stalking me. But that's ridiculous. I know I'm just worked up about my daughter starting school, and the funeral, and the news about Brad. Especially that.

"Yes, that's right. You must be Hannah Byers," I say, and the normal sound of my own voice breaks through the paranoia. "It's nice to meet you."

"Likewise," she says, stopping to take the hand I extend. Hers is very small, and very cold. "I have to say, I'm very excited to see this house."

She doesn't look excited. In fact, she looks almost terrified. But I've worked with plenty of nervous buyers, so there's nothing alarming about that, at least. "Well, I'm glad to hear it," I say. "This really is a fabulous home, with too many features to include in the listing. Do you want to wait for your agent? If not, we can go ahead and start looking around."

"My agent?" She blinks once. "I thought you were my agent. Aren't you the one selling this house?"

I press my lips together to keep the frown back. "I'm the listing agent. I work for the sellers," I say slowly. "Ms. Byers, is this your first time buying a home?"

"Please, it's Hannah." She looks confused, and more nervous than ever. "I just thought . . . I mean, no, I've never bought a house before. I didn't know I needed an agent." She gives a little sigh and takes her sunglasses off, tucking them into the bag slung over her shoulder. Her eyes are a startling blue, a shade almost as deep and vibrant as her car. She really is movie-star beautiful. "Can't you be my agent, too?" she says. "I really don't want to be bothered finding a different one. I just want to buy a house. Hopefully this one."

My throat goes a little dry, and I try not to think about the possibility of this working out. If she does retain me, and the sale goes through, I get the full six-percent commission instead of a fifty-fifty split. Twenty-four thousand dollars. But I have to be careful, because there are all sorts of rules about dual agency.

"Well . . . Hannah, I can represent you in the sale," I say in a measured tone. "But—"

"Perfect," she interrupts with a relieved smile. "You're my agent, then."

"But as a dual agent, I'll have to work with the best interests of the sellers in mind," I say anyway, because I'm required to. "Not that there's anything to disclose with this property. It's pretty straightforward. Still, you should be aware that a separate buyer's agent is recommended."

Hannah flaps a slim, expertly manicured hand at me. "You're fine. I trust you," she says. "I'm really good at reading people."

I'm almost proud of myself for hesitating before I reply. It's hard not to jump at the chance to double an already huge commission without considering the ethics, but I'm determined to do this all above-board.

"Okay. I'll just need you to sign an extra disclosure form, and I can represent you," I say. "Sound good?"

She smiles. "Fantastic, thank you. Can we look at the house?"

"Of course."

As I lead her across the walkway from the garage to the front door, my thoughts return to this morning and how out-of-place she seemed at the school, alone in a bathrobe with no child in evidence. I decide to poke at the mystery a little. "You know, this home is ideal for a big family," I say as I retrieve the house key from my purse and stop in front of the entrance. "Do you have any children?"

She doesn't answer right away. When I glance at her, there's a strange, almost distant look on her face. "I have a daughter," she says in a soft, halting tone. "Her name is Alice. She's four, but she'll be five in October. We . . . need a lot of space."

My breath catches, and I fumble the key as I'm trying to insert it in the deadbolt. It's just a coincidence, but it's a hell of a big one. "Wow, that's amazing," I manage in a normal voice, this time slipping the key home. "My daughter is four, and her birthday's in October too. Her name is Alyssa."

"Really?" Hannah flashes a smile that's almost painfully shy. "Maybe our daughters will be friends," she says. "See, I knew there was a reason I trusted you. This must be fate."

I'm not so sure about that, but at least I know she wasn't at the elementary school for no reason. Still, it's bizarre to think that she dropped her daughter off wearing a bathrobe and then stood there staring at the kids for who knows how long.

"Okay, here we go." I turn the key and open the door onto the grand foyer, ready to start my pitch. After all this time, if I finally manage to sell this house — and at double the commission — I'm definitely going to celebrate.

As I hold the door open for Hannah, I realize I've forgotten to ask about financing. And as a first-time homebuyer who thought she didn't need an agent, she probably didn't know much about the rest of the process either. "Hannah, do you have a pre-approval letter for the mortgage?" I say. "If you need help with financing, I can get you started with your bank or a lending company."

She gives another dismissive hand-wave. "Oh, I don't bother with things like that," she says. "I'll just pay cash."

"Cash?" I stammer, my dreams of a fat commission unraveling like smoke. Nobody pays the full asking price in cash, especially with a six-digit property. "Um. Well, unfortunately the sellers aren't willing to negotiate the price—"

"Four hundred thousand, right?" This time her smile is teasing, like a woman with a wicked secret. "Yes, I know. I've got it," she says. "I'm disgustingly rich, and I don't like to wait for what I want. I can pay the full price, in cash."

I hope she can't see the dollar signs dancing in my eyes as I follow her into the house.

CHAPTER 4

Alyssa talks a mile a minute about her day, all the way out of the school to the car. She's still talking when I pull onto the main road and head for home. I feel guilty for not hearing every word or responding as much as I should, because my head is still spinning.

Hannah Byers put in a purchase offer on the Victorian for four hundred thousand, cash, and the Quintaines accepted immediately. I'm selling the house.

I'm getting twenty-four thousand dollars.

"Mommy, did you hear me?" Alyssa says from the back seat.

I startle and blow out a long breath, trying to clear my head. This is a huge day for my daughter too, and she deserves my full attention. "I'm sorry, munchkin," I say. "I was tickling sheep."

She giggles at our private little joke. One of my mother's frequent sayings is 'I was woolgathering,' and I picked up the habit from her to brush off those spaced-out moments. The first time I said it to Alyssa, she wanted to know what it meant. I didn't know myself, exactly, and somehow from my rambling explanation, she boiled it down to 'tickling sheep.'

We'd both ended up on the floor, laughing like lunatics, and the expression stuck.

"Well, *stop* tickling them," she says, still giggling. "I said, I have a new best friend. Her name is Izzy. We ate lunch together, and we had pizza! She's really nice."

"That sounds awesome. The friend, and the pizza," I say, thinking suddenly of Hannah and her mystery daughter. "Can I ask you something, honey? Do you have a girl named Alice in your class?"

I glance in the rear-view mirror and catch my daughter's adorable, scrunched frown of concentration. "No," she says as she starts counting on her fingers. "There's Sophia, Lavender, Pammie, Dallas, Addison, Miguel . . ."

"Okay, okay," I laugh. "I get it. There's no Alice in your class."

"No Alice," she agrees. "I wish Izzy was in my class, though. She's in Miss Wilson's. Izzy says that Miss Wilson smells like a barn. What does a barn smell like, Mommy?"

I have to clap a hand over my mouth to keep from laughing. When I get control of myself, I say, "Barns smell like hay. Listen, honey . . . just so you know, it's not nice to tell people they smell like a barn. Okay?"

"Okay," she agrees cheerfully. "Mrs. Jocasta smells like pancakes."

Well, at least it's better than a barn.

Home is a nice three-bedroom, split-level white ranch with green trim, just six blocks from the elementary school. Maxine Hughes, the owner of the agency I work for, helped me get this place at an auction shortly after Alyssa was born, and I'm kind of proud of it. I've been luckier than most single mothers.

My heart clenches as I remember the news about Brad, and I pull into the garage trying to push the thought aside. I just can't deal with that tonight.

But I know I'll have to soon.

Alyssa waits until the engine turns off and the door unlocks, and then she springs from the car holding her backpack and races for the inside door to the kitchen. "I'm gonna win!" she shouts.

I take my time and let her win, gathering my purse and briefcase, then hitting the close button for the garage door on the way. By the time I reach the wooden steps, she's already inside, beaming triumphantly. "I won," she says. "Can I please have a Go-Gurt and some popcorn and watch cartoons?"

"Absolutely. Why don't you go put your backpack away in your room, and I'll meet you in the living room?"

"Yay!" She scrambles off into the house.

When I get inside, I set my stuff on the small table next to the door, then kick my shoes off and shove them under it. I'll get Alyssa's snack and then put everything away and change into something comfortable. The rest of today is cancelled, huge pending commission or not. I've already promised to spend it with my daughter.

I cross the kitchen, open a cabinet and grab a bag of popcorn, tearing the plastic wrap off before I toss it in the microwave and give it five minutes. That's way too long, but I don't trust the 'popcorn' button to stop the oven in time. I just listen for the pops to slow down.

My phone chimes in my pocket as I'm headed for the fridge, and I pull it out thinking I should set it on vibrate, or just turn it off. The notification is a text message. I debate ignoring it, but decide to check just this one before I make myself unavailable.

I tap through to my messages, and my heart drops in an unlovely swoop.

I know what you did. Murderer.

My mouth goes cotton dry. With shaking hands, I open the message, but there's no more. Just those six words. I don't recognize the number it came from, but the area code is Oslow. Where she lived.

A surge of helpless anger breaks through my panic, and I tap out, *Who the hell is this?* and hit send. I am *not* a murderer. She's dead, it's my fault and I have to live with that, but it wasn't murder.

22

Shivers run through me as I clench the phone almost tight enough to crack the screen, and I stare at it willing whoever this is to reply. I'm barely breathing and I can't seem to swallow. This can't be happening. Or maybe it's just a joke, an awful, tasteless prank sent to the wrong number.

My phone chimes again.

Wouldn't you like to know?

Oh, God. What am I supposed to do about this? Maybe I should call the police — but it's not exactly a threat, the way it's worded. Just an accusation.

It feels like a threat, though.

"Mommy? Are you okay?"

Somehow I manage not to scream at the sound of my daughter's voice, but I drop the phone and wince as it bounces on the tiled floor. "I'm fine, munchkin," I say without turning around, not wanting her to see my face until I calm down a little. I grab the phone and curse inwardly before I shove it in my pocket. The screen's cracked. "Everything okay with you?"

I turn to find her standing in the doorway between the kitchen and the dining room, her nose wrinkled in distaste. "It smells like a barn in here," she says.

That's when I finally notice the burning smell.

"Oh, no. The popcorn!" I rush to the microwave and yank the door open. Clouds of scorch-scented smoke billow out, and I cough and wave a hand in front of my face. "Stay back, honey," I say. "I have to make sure it's safe."

The smoke clears slowly. At least the bag isn't on fire, but it's blackened along the top and still smoldering. I grab the bottom edge, rush over to the sink, and run tap water over the whole bag. Steam hisses from the charred edges as the cold water drenches and shrivels everything.

And a small voice pipes up behind me: "Do I *have* to eat that popcorn, Mommy?"

The laugh that bursts from my throat is shrill and desperate, but at least it's a laugh. I lean down and pick up Alyssa, carrying her away from the sink. "No way. I'll make you a whole new bag," I say as I head through the dining room and into the living room. "One that doesn't smell like a barn."

I expect a giggle or a smile, but my daughter only looks at me, her small face serious. "You're so sad," she says. "It's okay. I don't need popcorn."

"Oh, honey." I stop beside the couch and hug her, breathing in the sweet smell of her hair. I have to force myself not to shake. "Trust me, popcorn is not a problem."

She squeezes me back and plants an unexpected kiss on my lips. "I love you."

"I love you, too. So much."

I swing her down to the couch, and she giggles as I tickle her. "Now serving popcorn and Go-Gurt in the living room," I say. "I'll be back in a few minutes."

I'm trembling as I head to the kitchen. As if Rosalie's suicide and Brad basically returning from the dead isn't enough, now I've got someone threatening me through text messages. And I have no idea what to do about any of it.

For now, I'm going to stick with the plan and spend the day with my daughter, having fun — or trying to. It's something I think we both need.

CHAPTER 5

It's day two of kindergarten, and Alyssa is already insisting that I don't have to walk her all the way to her classroom. I take her as far as the sidewalk past the buses, and she hugs me before she joins the throngs of kids flowing into the school. She's so small that I lose sight of her almost instantly, and I'm tempted to follow after her, just to make sure she's safe. But I head back to my car and drive to work instead.

I don't see Hannah at the school this morning, with or without the child who has so much in common with mine. Part of me wonders if she's lying about having a daughter. But I know I'm being ridiculous — why would she lie about that? Besides, there are four kindergarten classes at the school, so Alice Byers must be in one of the other three.

Today is going to be a little outside the norm. I'd called Jill last night after I got Alyssa tucked into bed and told her about my big sale. She was more excited than me and insisted that we go out for a quick drink tonight, even though it was a weekday. I *did* want to celebrate, but I'd feel guilty leaving my daughter. So we'd compromise. I'd get a sitter to come after Alyssa was asleep, and we'd hit Old City for an hour or so.

We'd talked briefly about Brad, and I told her I still hadn't decided what to do. I almost mentioned the disturbing text, but I changed my mind at the last minute. Telling Jill what I'd done wasn't at the top of my list of confessions I wanted to make. I was too ashamed to admit it to anyone.

But I have to put that out of my mind now. I'm almost at work.

The office of Hughes Real Estate is less than a mile from the elementary school. It's a small, one-story building that looks more like a house than a business, with a row of six parking spaces out front and a slightly larger parking lot in the back. I drive around back and park far from the building, reminding myself to focus on work, because it'll help me keep my mind off everything else for a while. Then I head inside. It's still early, not quite eight, but Maxine will be here. No one knows exactly how early she gets in, but it's always before everyone else.

The office is an open floor plan with most of the space dedicated to desks. Eight stations, each with a small, flimsy 'privacy wall' rather than traditional cubicles, and then a reception area by the front entrance and Maxine's private office at the back. Right now we only have four agents, plus Maxine and her niece, Courtney, whose job is to sit at the reception desk and work hard at avoiding work. She's the only one who isn't on commission, and the word hustle is definitely not in her vocabulary.

When I walk in, the main area is deserted and Maxine's door is closed, but her office lights are on and I can see her shape in there behind the frosted glass. I head for my desk, planning to spend the morning editing photos, updating my listings, and tackling any busywork I can find. I need a little down time after all that's happened.

As I'm sitting down to start my computer up, Maxine emerges with an empty mug and heads for the coffee counter behind the reception desk, giving me a nod of acknowledgment as she passes. She's one of those women who make aging seem effortless — at sixty-five, she looks fifty and acts forty. Today she's wearing a bright-print wrap skirt and a white top with a silver shimmer that matches her close-cropped hair, large silver hoop earrings, and a pretty turquoise pendant.

If she had a matching head wrap, she'd look like a fortune teller. But I'm not going to mention that. Maxine's breezy fashion sense suits her just fine.

She pours herself a cup of black coffee and turns back, slowing as she approaches me. "That's what I like to see. People chained to their desks first thing in the morning," she says with a teasing smile. "How's your daughter doing with school?"

"Great so far. She took right to it," I say.

"Good to hear." Maxine nods and sips at her coffee. "Great work on the Quintaine property, by the way. I really didn't think that one would ever sell."

I shake my head. "Same here."

"Well, it's in the bag now. Nicely done." She lifts her mug slightly in a half-salute, and then keeps walking toward her office without another word.

I figure that's her small-talk quota for the day. Maxine doesn't like to waste time.

By now my computer's finished cycling to life, and I get started on all the tedious, mundane tasks that require a lot of time but not much attention. An hour passes before I know it, and I only notice the time when the back door opens and someone walks in. I glance up and then look away fast, hoping I didn't make eye contact.

Sabrina Groth is not my favorite person in the world.

Damn, she's coming toward me. I hold back a sigh and look up, pasting on a smile that's as phony as they come, but I don't care if she notices. Sabrina is the top-selling agent in the company and makes sure everyone knows it. She's the competitive type, and for some reason she's decided that I'm her main competition.

But she never seems to get that she's only winning the game because I'm not playing.

"Good morning, Sabrina," I say when she stops in front of my desk. "I like your sweater."

I don't actually. It's pink and fuzzy, probably angora, and it reminds me of Dolores Umbridge from the Harry

Potter movies. Come to think of it, Sabrina basically is Umbridge — all outward sweetness and light, with a nasty undertone to every word she utters.

I'm waiting for her to say something like 'oh, this old thing?', but she doesn't. She gets right down to business. "Hello, Celine. I hear you found a buyer for the Quintaine place," she says with a brittle smile. "Congratulations. It must've been a fluke, like winning the lottery."

Maybe it was, but I won't give her the satisfaction of agreeing. "Did you need something, Sabrina? I have work to do."

"Do you?" Her smile curls up like the Cheshire cat as she leans back and inspects her blood-red nails. "I thought you'd be at the hospital today. You know . . . with Brad," she says. "Weren't you with him before the accident? I mean, he probably still thinks you're his girlfriend."

My jaw clenches hard. "I think Brad has enough problems right now," I say.

"Really. So you're a problem?" she says sweetly, blinking innocent eyes at me. "You had him the longest, even though he was probably cheating on you, too. I never understood why you stayed." She leans forward and stage-whispers, "He's really not that good in bed. I only had him twice, before I gave up on him."

"Well, Sabrina, everybody else thought he was a great fuck. So maybe the problem was you," I fire back before I can think about it. I really shouldn't be surprised that Brad was with Sabrina. He'd moved to Wolfsbrook during his senior year, when I was a junior, and he'd still managed to screw most of his class and half of mine before he graduated — or at least it seemed that way. The big, handsome football hero. Then he'd moved on to screw his way through college.

And yeah, I was the last one before the accident and the coma. But I'd been with him for a year, and . . .

I'm not going to think about that.

Sabrina only looks shocked for a second. She straightens and recovers with a sanguine smile. "You poor thing. You must've been a virgin before Brad," she says. "Have you been waiting all this time for him? You *really* don't know what you're missing."

My phone vibrates, saving me from saying something really nasty. I pull it out and see Hannah Byers' number on the screen. "Excuse me, I have to take this," I say, giving back all of her saccharine sweetness and then some. "It's the Quintaine buyer. You know, the fluke?"

Thunderheads form in her eyes, and she pivots on a heel and stalks across the room to her desk.

I have to resist an overwhelming urge to stick my tongue out at her as I answer the call. "Good morning, this is Celine."

"Hi, it's Hannah. I'm buying a house from you?" she says uncertainly.

A smile twitches across my mouth. This is like calling Domino's and saying, 'I'm the one who ordered a pizza.' "Yes, Hannah, hello," I say. "I remember you. Can I help you with something?"

She pauses, and I hear a quick intake of breath. "I was just wondering if I'd be able to move in soon," she says. "I know there's more paperwork, but can we do that today? I'd love to move tomorrow."

Oh, my stars and garters. It's another of my mom's favorite sayings, and it's all I can think to describe my reaction. She really is completely clueless. "Well," I say slowly, "closing on a house usually takes four to six weeks. But since this is a cash sale, it shouldn't take that long. I'd plan on about two weeks, total."

"Two weeks?" she says with real dismay. "Oh, no, that's far too long. Can't we do it faster?"

I frown and notice Sabrina smirking at me from across the room, like a lion catching the scent of a wounded gazelle, so I force a smile. Apparently this property is going to give me trouble right through the bitter end. "Tell you what," I say. "I'll make some calls, and I might be able to push things up to first thing next week."

Hannah gusts a relieved breath. "Really? That would be so much better. Will Monday work, do you think?"

"That's what I'll aim for," I tell her. Today is Tuesday. The longest part of the process, other than mortgage processing which Hannah doesn't need, is usually waiting on the lawyers — but Jill is a paralegal at the firm we normally work with, and hopefully she'll help me fast-track this one. "I'm sorry it can't be sooner, but—"

"Monday is fine," she says brusquely, as if she hadn't just been panic-stricken when I told her she couldn't move in tomorrow. "Thank you so much, Celine. You'll keep me updated, won't you?"

"Yes, of course."

I manage to get in a goodbye before she hangs up, and I stare at the phone for a moment, shaking my head. Hannah seems . . . a bit eccentric. But maybe this is normal for her. I've never met an actual rich person before, so who knew. They might all be like this.

"Is something wrong, Celine?" Sabrina calls out, looking terribly concerned.

"Not a thing," I say as I swipe to my address book and pull up Jill's office number. I find myself wondering if this sale will put me ahead of Sabrina in commissions, if that's why she's coming at me so hard, and smile at the idea. Serves her right if it does.

Tuning out the woman who would be queen of real estate, I dial Jill and open my email on the computer, so I can forward her the contract. She answers on the second ring with, "Jeff Lindstrom's office, can I help you?"

"Hey, it's me," I say.

"Morning, hon. Wait a second," she says. "You're not calling to cancel drinks tonight, are you? Because I already need one."

I laugh. "That kind of day, huh? No, I'm not cancelling."

"Good. I've got the biggest rant ever for you later," she says. "What's up?"

"Actually, I need a favor if you have time," I say as I start scrolling through my inbox for the contract. "On the Quintaine sale, the one we're celebrating. The buyer is — oh, what the hell is this?" I break off as I see an email from the New Hampshire Real Estate Commission about renewing my license. The bar is shaded like it's already been clicked on and read, but I don't remember reading it.

"What happened?" Jill says. "Don't tell me something went wrong already."

"No, it's not that," I mutter as I click on the email, which informs me that my license is going to expire in seven days. But the message is dated last Friday, so it's actually expiring in three days. How could I have missed this? I'll have to take care of it right away. "Apparently my license is expiring," I say.

"Your driver's license?"

"My real estate license. I thought it was . . . well, whatever. I'll just do it," I say, opening the renewal link in a new tab and then going back to my inbox. "Anyway, I was wondering if you could get this contract reviewed fast. Like, maybe today? The buyer is highly motivated."

Jill snorts a laugh. "I thought that's what you're supposed to say about sellers," she says, typing rapidly in the background. "Sure, no problem. Send it through and I'll make sure you have it by this afternoon."

"You're amazing. Thank you."

"Hey, I'm super-paralegal. Able to leap tall filing deadlines in a single bound, no matter how many weeks certain people who aren't even my boss have failed to tell me about the aforementioned deadlines," she says with cutting sarcasm. Now I know exactly what she's going to rant about tonight: Danny Voltaire, the firm's newest junior partner, who's been a six-month thorn in Jill's side. The kind of guy who'd forget his own head if it wasn't attached. I don't imagine that extreme forgetfulness is a good quality for a lawyer to have.

"Can't wait to hear this one," I say with a smirk. "Thanks again, Jill. I'm sending the contract now."

After a few seconds, she says, "Okay, got it. Talk to you later — I have to run over to the courthouse for some mysteriously immediate reason."

"Yeah, I wonder what that is?"

That gets her laughing. We say goodbye and hang up, and I see Lucas Turow coming in from the back, burdened with a shoulder bag, a briefcase, and a bunch of signs under one arm. Speaking of people who aren't exactly organized. But Lucas is a decent guy — and with another agent around, Sabrina will cool her heels. She saves her worst snark for one-on-one sessions with whoever's lucky enough to be alone with her.

I wave good morning to Lucas and go back to my computer, tabbing over from my email to the license renewal form. I should've had another full year before I needed to renew, but with the closing on the Quintaine property coming up so fast, I don't want to bother arguing with the real estate commission. I'll just fill this out and pay the eighty bucks and then worry about disputing it next week. They take forever to do anything.

For some reason my auto-fill isn't working, and I have to type in all my information separately. But my computer is dragging, the cursor blinking too fast and the letters lagging behind my keystrokes. It's not a big deal, just annoying. I chalk it up to everything about this property being a huge pain in the ass.

I can't wait to close and get it out of my life.

CHAPTER 6

Alyssa's second day of school was apparently even more exciting than the first, now that she's had pizza for lunch two days in a row with Izzy. From the way my daughter talks about her new friend, Izzy might be the second coming of Christ. But I'm glad she's happy.

I have her in bed by eight, and she's sound asleep before the sitter gets there at nine. I'm glad Tabitha Foster is available tonight. She's been Alyssa's regular sitter since my daughter was a baby, and I thought she'd left for college a few weeks ago, but it turns out she's not starting until the winter semester. Tabitha knows my numbers and where everything is in the house, so it's just a matter of saying hello and thanking her before I head out.

It's almost nine-thirty when I get to Old City, the most popular of the three bars in Wolfsbrook. The place is the last building on a dead-end street at the 'waterfront' of Saginaw Creek, a fat ribbon of dark-green water that no one would dare swim in but everyone loves to look at. There's plenty of parking available tonight, since it's the middle of the week, so I grab a spot and head inside.

Jill is already at the bar. She stands and waves when I come in, like I don't see her in the bright-green top and white yoga pants she's wearing. I can't get away with outfits like that anymore, but she looks amazing as always.

The bartender she was talking to walks off, and Jill squeals a little as she hugs me. "Oh my God, you're gonna be rich!" she says. "How does it feel?"

"Unbelievable." I laugh and take the stool next to her. I've been spending too much time figuring out how much I'll actually get — about fifteen thousand, after taxes and agency fees — and what I'll do when I get it. So far all I know for sure is that I'm finally getting a remote starter installed in my car for winter, and Alyssa is going to have the most amazing fifth birthday ever. "I tell you, though. After two years, I feel like I made about three bucks an hour on this."

"You think way too much, do you know that?"

Jill smiles and elbows me, grabbing my hand as I start to wave for the bartender. "I already ordered you a Tom Collins," she says as she wiggles the nearly full glass on the counter in front of her. "Got mine right here, all ready for a toast."

"Perfect."

It's not long before the bartender brings my drink, and as I take it with a nod of thanks, Jill lifts her glass. "Let's see," she says, striking an exaggerated thinking pose. "Here's to Celine, she's a good old bean."

"Old bean?" I arch an eyebrow. "Here's to Jill, she's quite a thrill."

Jill's lips twitch. "Here's to Celine, she's rich but not mean."

"Here's to Jill not falling down a hill."

We both dissolve into laughter and clink our glasses together. I still feel a little guilty leaving Alyssa, like I always do, but it's good to be here. To be me for a while, and not just Alyssa's mom.

Jill launches into her latest story about Danny Voltaire and his incompetence, and I listen and laugh and drink until I'm pleasantly buzzed. Eventually we order cheese sticks and move to a side table. I find myself thinking about the past, about college and all those nights like this — only much later and with more people — and Brad's face fills my mind like an accusation.

"Jill," I say into a moment of comfortable silence. "I've got to do something about Brad."

Concern fills her face, and she sighs as she toys with a half-eaten cheese stick. "I can't believe he's awake," she says. "I mean, five years. That has to be some kind of record."

I swallow back unpleasant laughter. Brad Dowling probably broke a lot of records, on the football field and in the bedroom. He also broke a lot of hearts, including mine. As the absolutely gorgeous, only son of incredibly wealthy parents, everyone wanted him — and he often wanted everyone right back. It honestly wouldn't surprise me if he'd cheated on me during the year we'd been together.

But I still love him. God help me, after all this time and all the energy I've spent actively not thinking about him, I still love him.

And there's something he has to know.

"I have to tell him," I say aloud, mostly to convince myself. "Don't I?"

Jill gives me a sympathetic smile. "Maybe not yet," she says. "He's probably really weak and he's going to need a lot of physical therapy, after five years in bed. He'll be confused about everything. Plus, he might have brain damage."

"Brain damage?" I echo. "Wait, how do you know all this stuff?"

She smirks. "I did a little research on coma patients. Morbid curiosity."

"Oh, God. What if he does have brain damage?" I say in a cracked whisper. "What if he's awake, and I still can't tell him about . . ."

I don't even realize I'm crying until Jill reaches across the table and squeezes my hand. I jump a little, startling a tear down my cheek. "It's only been a few days," she says gently. "Give it time. He probably has a lot of people throwing a lot of things at him right now, especially his parents."

The thought of Willa and Bennett Dowling leaves me cold. They're the reason I stopped visiting Brad a few weeks after the accident, and eventually stopped believing he'd wake up. I have no idea how they found out about the argument we had that night, since I'd never told anyone and Brad couldn't. They must've known someone at the restaurant.

However it happened, Willa Dowling had made her feelings about me crystal clear to the entire fourth floor of Hayhurst Memorial Hospital.

"Celine?" a somewhat familiar voice says, dragging me from the memory of Willa's red, contorted face and shrill screams. "That is you, isn't it?"

I blink and find myself looking at Hannah Byers, who's standing next to our table with a full wine glass in one hand and an unlit cigarette in the other. She's wearing a glittering gold cocktail dress and a white sash that says *Bead Babe*, and there are feathers stuck in her hair. I'm not sure what look she's going for, but I'm pretty sure she hasn't achieved it. I guess she's so gorgeous that it doesn't really matter.

She's also out at a bar, alone, on a school night. Interesting.

"Hi, Hannah," I finally say, flashing an apologetic smile at Jill. "Uh, this is my friend Jill. Jill, this is Hannah Byers. She's buying the Quintaine house."

"Well, it's the Byers house now, isn't it?" Hannah says with a slightly brittle smile, but her expression smoothes as she nods in greeting. She doesn't offer a hand, though — they're both full. "Nice to meet you, Jill."

"You too," Jill says, looking bemused as her gaze travels Hannah's outfit. "I hear you're getting a lot of house."

"The most my money can buy here," Hannah agrees cheerfully. "I think I'm going to like Wolfsbrook. This is only the second bar I've been in tonight, and I've already found someone I know. It's what happens in small towns, right?" She drops me a conspiratorial wink, as if we're suddenly best friends sharing a secret. "How long have you two lived here?"

Jill and I exchange a glance. Only the second bar? If she's expecting to find a lot of thriving nightlife in Wolfsbrook to choose from, she's going to be disappointed. "I grew up here," I say. "And Jill's been here since college. She's from Oslow."

"Really? I'm from Oslow too. Well . . . sort of," Hannah says with the same strange, distant look that came over her when she talked about her daughter. She shakes herself and smiles again. "I'm going outside to smoke. The bartender says there's a great view of the river from the back. See you later, ladies."

She walks off, weaving a little as she heads for the back door that leads to the patio. I stare after her until she's outside, and then I clap a hand over my mouth to keep a laugh from escaping.

Jill doesn't bother holding back, and soon I'm laughing right along with her. I'm not usually the type to make fun of people — but I've never met anyone like Hannah.

"I think there's something wrong with her," Jill says. "You know, like . . ." She trails off and twirls a finger around her ear.

"Yeah, maybe." I calm down and sip at my drink. "But she's also insanely rich, so I guess she's allowed to be a little cuckoo for Cocoa Puffs." That sets Jill off again, and I laugh with her for a minute. "Seriously, though? I think she has a pretend daughter."

Jill frowns. "What do you mean?"

I tell her about seeing Hannah at the school that morning and point out that she's here alone on a school night. At least I have the excuse of being out with a friend. And I explain the little Hannah's told me — that her daughter is four, turning five in October, and her name is Alice. I even say that Alyssa doesn't have an Alice in her class and hasn't met any kindergartners named Alice.

The more I talk, the worse I feel about myself. I can't believe I'm sitting here gossiping like a mean girl about a woman I hardly know. And I'm stretching the facts to fit some half-formed narrative that's too crazy to be true.

But Jill is into it, wide-eyed and nodding along. "That's so insane," she says. "I mean, even the name is almost the same. Alice, Alyssa. It's like she made up a daughter just so she'd have something in common with you. Did you tell her about Alyssa before or after she mentioned this?"

"She, uh . . ." Suddenly I can't remember. Who mentioned which child first? I try to mentally replay meeting Hannah at the Quintaine property, remember the conversation before we went into the house. "She was first," I finally say.

Jill raises her brow. "Are you sure?"

"Positive." I nod, confirming it to myself. "I asked her if she had any kids, because she was looking at this huge house by herself, and she told me all this stuff about her daughter. Then I said wow, that's just like my daughter."

"Celine," Jill says carefully. "Maybe she knew about Alyssa before she talked to you."

My blood runs icy cold, and I squeeze my eyes shut against a pulse of panic. But that's a truly insane idea. Total paranoia. I'm not going to give in to that, especially since I've already embellished a lot of my 'logic' that points to Hannah having a made-up child. I'm sure Alice is real. "No, she couldn't have," I say. "She doesn't know anything about me, or Alyssa."

Jill makes her eyes wide and waggles her fingers in the air. "Unless she's rich . . . *and psychic*," she intones. "Look into my crystal ball, dahling. Madame Bead Babe sees all."

I choke on a laugh, and soon we're both giggling. I guess I'm a little more buzzed than I thought.

Things will look better tomorrow.

CHAPTER 7

At least I'm not hung over the next morning. But I've got a lot on my mind when I take Alyssa to school, and I give her an extra-long hug on the sidewalk before she goes inside. She squirms out of it impatiently, smacking a kiss on my cheek before she runs off to join her friends.

I watch her growing up so fast, and I know I have to tell Brad. I can't put it off.

There's no way I can make this call from the office. I don't want to be alone at home, either, because I'm going to have an emotional reaction no matter what happens. Maybe if I'm out in public, I won't have a complete breakdown.

I head for the Coffee Stop Café, all the way across downtown from the real estate office. For some reason I don't want anyone to know what I'm doing, as if contacting the man I once thought I'd marry is some kind of dirty secret. But there's so much about Brad and me that no one knows, sometimes it feels that way. Like a secret I'm ashamed to tell.

I have too many of those.

The café is on a corner lot next to an office building, which means it's likely to be fairly busy even this early in the morning. I park at the curb on the side street and leave my briefcase in the car, walking inside to join the line of impatient people waiting for their morning dose of caffeine. It takes fifteen minutes for me to reach the register and place my order, but only a few before my name is called and I'm handed a hazelnut cappuccino and a blueberry muffin on a plastic tray.

I find an empty table for two near the front windows and sit down, slowly tuning out the noise and chatter of the café while I stare outside at the passing cars and the pretty facade of this town. I never thought I'd be here, doing . . . this. I was supposed to get out. From the college in the city, where I'd been working on a degree in photography and digital cinematography, I'd planned bigger and better things. With Brad. Maybe after college we'd move to Nashau, where he lived before he came to Wolfsbrook, or maybe we'd head to New York City or even California. Somewhere fun and exciting. But then the argument happened, and the accident. From that point on, he had to be dead to me. It was the only way I could deal with the aftermath.

I love my daughter more than life itself, and I wouldn't trade her for anything. Not even all those dreams I used to have. But she wasn't exactly planned.

And her father has no idea she exists.

My hands shake slightly as I take out my phone and stare at it. I still need a few more minutes. I take a sip of my cooling coffee, tap the screen and swipe my password, then pull up my texts out of habit. The message at the bottom catches my eye, the last reply from the unknown number: *Wouldn't you like to know?* Yes, I think bitterly, I *would* like to know who you are. I haven't received any more veiled threats since this brief exchange, and I should probably delete the message and forget about the mystery nutcase who sent it, but I don't want to erase the evidence.

Especially since I don't know what it's evidence of.

I frown and swipe away from the text screen, then open my Firefox app and tap to Google. As I start entering Hayhurst in the search bar, the full name of the hospital pops up and I select it before I can change my mind. The main result includes a linked phone number for hospital information. I take a breath, tap the number and hold the phone to my ear.

After two rings, a pleasant female voice answers. "Hayhurst Memorial Hospital, how may I direct your call?"

My stomach twists, and I almost hang up. I don't want to do this. "Hello," I stammer anyway. "I'm looking for a patient, I think. Brad Dowling?"

"I can help you with that. One moment," the woman says, and I hear her typing in the background. After a minute she says, "I have his room number and direct phone line. Would you like that information?"

"Uh, yes. Please. Just let me . . ." I dig in my purse for a pen, and then grab the café receipt I stuffed in my pocket and smooth it out on the table. "Okay, go ahead."

She tells me he's in room 548 — apparently he's been moved up a floor — and then reads off a phone number. I write everything down. When she's finished, I say quietly, "Can you tell me how he's doing?"

"Well, I can transfer you to the fifth-floor nurse's station," she says. "I'm not sure how much they'll be able to share, but you can ask."

"Okay. Thank you."

There's a click, and the line buzzes a few times before another woman answers. "Fifth floor," she says.

"Hello," I begin, but then I hesitate, not sure what I'm going to ask. Or if I want to hear the answer. Finally I say, "I was wondering if you could tell me about Brad Dowling. If he's . . . awake."

After a brief pause, the woman says, "Are you family?"

"No. I'm sorry." I have no idea why I apologize for that.

"I can only give out patient updates to family members," she says. But her voice softens as she asks, "Are you a friend of his?"

My heart lurches. The news is either very good, or very bad. "Yes, I'm a friend," I say. "I want to visit him, but I don't know if he's . . ."

When I don't finish, the woman speaks with a smile in her voice. "That should be just fine," she says. "Our visiting hours are from 10 a.m. to 9 p.m. And frankly, Mr. Dowling is doing miraculously well, though you'll have to ask him for any details you'd like to know."

"Thank you," I say, not sure whether I'm relieved or afraid. Probably both. "I guess I'll just call his room, then. I have the number."

"All right, dear. You do that."

I say goodbye and end the call, staring at the stark black numbers I've scribbled on the back of the white receipt. Brad is at the other end of those numbers — alive, awake, and 'miraculously well.' After all this time. I just can't believe it, and I might not even after I hear his voice. I'm torn between what's easy and what's right.

After a long five minutes of indecision, I dial the number.

The phone rings three times before someone says, "Hello?" The voice is an older woman, and I close my eyes and pray it's a nurse, even though I know it must be Willa Dowling. Still the mother bear to a child who's nearly thirty.

"Mrs. Dowling?" I half-whisper. "I was wondering if I could . . . talk to Brad." Maybe she won't ask for my name.

"Well, I don't know. He's barely awake yet." I hear a rasping voice in the background, raised in faint protest, and tears spring hot to my eyes. *Brad*. Oh God, it's true. I still recognize him in that weak, awful murmur, even though I can't make out a word he says.

I have a pretty good idea, though.

It's on the tip of my tongue to say I'll call back later, but if I wait much longer I'll lose my nerve. "If it's okay with Brad, I'd really like to speak to him," I say. "Please."

"Who is this?" Willa nearly barks.

Damn it. I consider using someone else's name, or making one up, but I know I'll have to confront him face-to-face soon. I need him to know that I tried to call before I spring what may be the biggest shock of his life on him.

"It's Celine," I say. "Celine Bauman."

Absolute, frigid silence responds.

"Mrs. Dowling?"

"You little *bitch*," Willa hisses suddenly in a strained voice.

My breath catches, and the tears start flowing as I absorb what feels like a physical slap. I'd expected anger, but this is undiluted hatred.

"How dare you?" Her voice rises to that shrill tone I remember from the last time I saw Brad, when he'd already been unconscious for two weeks and I thought that was a long time. "You are not entitled to speak to my son, do you hear me? I won't have you upsetting him after he's finally come back to me!"

Mom! Who is it? This time I make out the background words, delivered in a ragged gasp that's painful to hear.

"If you come near him, I'll kill you."

Willa Dowling speaks those words with a terrifying flat inflection, and then hangs up.

Just like the first time I heard Brad was awake, I can't breathe. The phone clatters from my numb hand and falls on the table, and I stare at nothing as my eyes flood and my chest burns. God, this can't be happening. What am I going to do?

I don't know how long I've been sitting there when a hand brushes my shoulder, and I nearly jump out of my skin. Figuring it's a concerned employee, I turn my face away and grab a napkin to swipe at my eyes. I'm probably smearing mascara all over myself. I heave a shaking breath, grab another napkin and try to determine the best way to head for the bathroom.

"Celine, honey, are you okay?" a voice says.

I blink in surprise and turn to see Missy Wilson standing there, with a blond-haired young man I don't recognize hovering nervously behind her. "I, er . . . hi, Missy," I mutter inanely. Of all the people to catch me bawling, it had to be her. "What are you doing here?"

"Oh, I always come here in the mornings. They make a fabulous mocha espresso," she says breezily, and then slides uninvited into the chair across from me, leaving her companion to stand awkwardly alone. She leans across the table and arranges her face into something like sympathy. "It always hits at the worst times, doesn't it?" she says. "Poor Rosalie. I'm still in shock, myself."

My airways loosen a little. I'm more than happy to let her think I'm crying for Rosalie, because she's the last person I want to talk to about Brad. "Yes, it's just terrible. Poor Rosalie," I say as I grab a clean napkin and mop blindly at my face. "I'm sorry I left early the other day."

"Don't worry. I understand, with Brad and everything." Missy unzips the little clutch purse at her side and hands me a compact and a single-wrapped moist facial wipe. "Here you go, honey. I've practically bought stock in these things since the day I heard, so just shout if you need more than one."

I'm surprised and a little touched by the gesture. "Thank you," I say, and open the compact. When I get a look at myself in the mirror, I blurt out a watery laugh. The hollows under my eyes are smudged completely black, like the grease football players wear, and black lines radiate down my cheeks. "Oh, my God. I think I might need more than one."

"Well, I didn't want to mention that you look awful." Missy laughs a little as she ducks her head to go through her purse again, and I catch the shine in her own eyes. She takes out two more pre-moistened wipes and looks away briefly before she puts them on the table.

It's obvious that no matter what she acts like, she's truly devastated by Rosalie's death.

I clean myself up in silence, half afraid to say something that might set us both off. When I hand the compact back to her, she smiles, a little more in control. "Have you met my fiancé?" she says, gesturing at the blond guy who's still hovering around like he's not sure where to stand.

Fiancé? I'm pretty sure that Missy had gotten married right after college to some older man she met there. But maybe I'd heard wrong — or maybe things just didn't work out for them. Either way, I wouldn't bring it up. "No, I don't think I have," I say, turning a polite smile toward the blond. "Hello. I'm Celine Bauman."

The man clears his throat and smiles. "Dan Voltaire," he says. "Hello."

I can feel my eyes trying to bug out and work to keep my features neutral. Danny Voltaire, the world's most scatter-brained lawyer and the bane of Jill's existence, is engaged to Missy Wilson. Oh, boy. I can't wait to tell Jill about this one.

"Dan and I were just stopping by for coffee before he goes to work," Missy says almost apologetically as she stands. "But then I saw you, and . . . well, I just wanted to make sure you were okay."

"Thank you. I'm glad you did," I say with genuine warmth, getting up myself. "It's fine, I have to go to work too. Thanks for the wet wipes."

"Any time," Missy says, and hugs me. This time I hug her back.

Once she and Dan leave the café, I gather my stuff and head to the bathroom. I need to wash my face and touch up my makeup before I go to the office, and I'm still more shaken than I want to be. I feel bad about Rosalie all over again, especially when I remember the bizarre suicide note. The one that claimed she couldn't live without Brad.

And I can't help wondering whether Brad knew that.

CHAPTER 8

Life has been strangely normal for the past few days. Not that I want to complain about things being normal, but a return to the status quo means I haven't done anything more about Brad. I admit it: I'm terrified of his mother. I absolutely believe she might try to kill me. If anyone ever hurt Alyssa, I might do the same thing.

I'm even starting to think that maybe she's the one who sent that text.

But today, it's all quiet on the Bauman front. Alyssa still loves school, and I'm still pinching myself every time I remember that big commission I've got coming. I'm at the office, it's around ten in the morning, and Sabrina and I are the only ones here — not counting Courtney at the reception desk, who ignores everyone anyway. Even the looming possibility that my co-worker might wind up the snark-wagon at any moment doesn't bother me, though.

Right now, I am the world's okay-est real estate agent.

As I'm passively browsing the MLS, looking for potential matches for one of my sellers while I daydream about the money, my phone rings. The caller is in my address book — it's one of the two home inspectors I usually work with, the one who's doing the final inspection for the Quintaine property. I answer hoping for good news, and I get it. His report is finished and sitting in my inbox. Everything's good to go.

We can close on Monday.

I'm smiling as I dial Hannah. The phone rings four times, and then I get a voicemail message — just a standard, prerecorded 'the person you are calling is not available, please leave a message after the tone.' For a second I think it's strange, because she's been immediately available every time I've spoken to her.

Then I realize that I've never actually called her. She called me first to ask about the house and has preemptively called me to check in on things every time since.

The voicemail tone sounds, and I give my name and ask her to call me. But just as I set my phone on the desk, it rings and Hannah's number flashes on the screen.

Okay. That's exceedingly weird.

"Hello, Hannah?" I say as I answer. "I must've just missed you."

"Oh, no. I never answer calls," she says almost breathlessly. "I don't trust them."

I'm not sure what to say to that. I think 'eccentric' might be too mild a word for this woman.

"I'm so sorry. I said something strange, didn't I?" Hannah gives a nervous laugh. "I guess I still need to work on my sense of humor. It's not very good. Honestly, I was in the bathroom when you called. What I said was just a silly thing from a movie."

I don't know if I believe that, but I decide to let it drop. I only have to deal with her until Monday, and then I'll never see her again. "Well, I called to tell you that everything's ready for Monday," I say. "If you can be here at the office by 1 p.m. with your cashier's check, we'll go over and sign the paperwork. It'll take about an hour, and you'll leave with the keys to the house."

"Really?" Hannah says, sounding delighted. "That's wonderful. I'm so excited! Celine, will you . . ." She trails off and clears her throat. "I'm sorry. This is embarrassing, but I wondered if you'd come and have a drink with me tomorrow night, to celebrate. At that bar where I saw you and your friend. I . . . I don't know anyone else in town," she finishes in a small voice.

I absolutely want to turn her down. But she sounds so pathetic, and I know she's telling the truth — about this, at least. She really doesn't know anyone else. Besides, I only have to keep up being friendly until Monday, and then she'll move into her big house with all her money and do whatever rich people do.

"Sure, we can do that," I say. "Do you mind if Jill comes with us?" I almost feel bad asking that, but I'm not sure I want to be alone with Hannah. Tons of awkward potential there.

"Your friend? Not at all." She's so relieved, I can hear it in her breathing. "Maybe we can meet there at nine?"

"That works for me. See you then."

We hang up, and I smirk at the phone for a moment. Hannah really is something — I just wish I knew what. Now I have to call Tabitha to make sure she's available tomorrow night to watch Alyssa, and Jill to make sure she'll come with me. But before I can do any of that, I notice Sabrina stalking across the room toward my desk, spoiling for a catfight.

I imagine myself making some outrageous remark just to shut her up before she gets started, like 'What's wrong, Sabrina, did your plastic surgeon tell you he can't fix stupid?' Instead, like always, I paste on my fake smile and wait for her to drop the gauntlet.

It's not a long wait. She stops in front of me and drawls, "So you're finally closing the deal, are you? Took you long enough. I mean, if I had a property like that, I could've sold it in a week."

"Yes, well, we can't all be perfect like you," I fire back. It's the closest I dare to get to what I really want to say, and even speaking those words out loud makes me shaky. "Listen, Sabrina, I've got a lot of work—"

"Oh, I'll bet you do." She isn't going to back off. "By the way, have you been to see Brad yet? I have," she says. "His parents were *so* happy to see me. In fact, I'm thinking of giving him another chance."

"You're so full of shit!" I shout, startling myself — and Courtney, who glances over briefly from the reception desk before she goes back to playing on her phone. "You don't care about him," I say in a lower voice. "Go ahead and be the queen of real estate if you want to, but stop dragging Brad into whatever this is between us. He's been through enough."

Sabrina lunges and smacks her palms on my desk, leaning toward me with a shark's grin. "You're right. I don't care about Brad," she says. "*You*, on the other hand . . . I'm going to get rid of you."

"Excuse me?"

"You heard me." Her expression turns frosty. "I'm tired of busting my ass around here, just to watch you land the easy scores. I mean, how did you pull off a cash deal on a four-hundred-grand property? *Nobody* does that."

I'm actually a little scared now. She looks deranged. "I just got lucky. Right place, right time," I say in what I hope is a calm voice, glancing around to see whether Courtney is paying attention. Of course, she isn't. "Sabrina, what's this all about?"

The back door opens then, and Maxine bustles in with a cup of coffee in one hand and a box of donuts in the other. Sabrina backs off instantly, all smiles for the boss, but there's a predatory gleam in her eyes.

"Happy Friday. Don't say I never got you anything," Maxine says as she crosses the room to deposit the donut box on the counter next to the coffee pot. If she notices the tension in the room, she doesn't mention it.

Courtney makes a beeline for the donuts. I wouldn't mind one, but I'm not ready to move just yet. I'm still shaken by Sabrina's outburst.

"You're the best, Maxine," Sabrina says. "Wish I could have one, but I've got to run. I have an open house this afternoon and I'm expecting at least half a dozen offers."

Maxine rolls her eyes slightly. "Good for you," she says, already heading toward her office. "Hope you don't sprain your arm too hard patting yourself on the back."

I manage to clamp my mouth shut over a laugh, but it's close.

At least Maxine's presence has taken the air out of Sabrina's sails. She heads stiffly to her desk, grabs her purse and briefcase, and turns to look at me. "Enjoy being on top while you can," she says with syrupy sweetness. "You won't stay there long."

I shake my head as she walks to the back door and leaves the building. Whatever's gotten into her, she'll probably get over it once the closing is over and she has more amazing sales to boast about. I won't be much competition for a while. I'm already planning to coast on my little windfall, at least for a few weeks, while I deal with other things. Like Brad.

Once Sabrina is gone, my heart rate finally settles somewhere around normal. I grab my phone to call Tabitha about tomorrow night. But it chimes in my hand as a text comes in, and my nice, normal heartbeat stops entirely.

You don't deserve the life you have.

It's from the same unknown number as the one accusing me of murder. Shivering, I tap on the message bubble, and another text chimes in as the thread opens.

I'm going to take it from you.

"What the hell?" I say aloud, hitting the reply box. I'm half tempted to go out to the back parking lot and see if Sabrina is sitting in her car on her phone, but I tap out a reply instead. *Is this you, Sabrina?*

I send the message and wait. Eventually, the phone pings again.

It's not going to be that easy. You'll never see me coming.

I'm cold all over and wondering whether I should call the police after all. This definitely sounds like a threat. I just don't know what they're threatening.

But I have a sinking feeling I'm going to find out.

CHAPTER 9

Alyssa is thrilled about Tabitha coming over tonight. Since it's not a school night, she gets to stay up late and watch movies and be goofy. She's in her pajamas on the couch, and I'm next to her in my going-out clothes — boots and black jeans, a lacy cream-colored top, and a long, lightweight cardigan with big pockets.

My daughter works the remote, navigating Netflix with frightening ease. I don't recall being this easy with technology at four years old. But then, who remembers being four? My first memory is turning eight and feeling angry because my parents bought my little sister a present for my birthday so she wouldn't feel left out. They never got *me* a present for *her* birthday. I remember thinking I'd confront my mom, and then playing out the conversation in my head: *Why does Vivian get a present for my birthday, but I don't get one for hers? Because you're the big sister, Celine. You have to be responsible, and Vivian is too little to understand why she doesn't get any presents. But she's five, Mom. She does understand. It's not fair. Well, if it's not fair, then we'll just take all the presents back to the store and no one will get any.*

That exchange never took place, because after I thought about it, I decided not to complain. Even then I was afraid of confrontation.

Now Vivian's in California, studying structural engineering at UC Berkeley — and I'm still here, disappointing my mother. She's never been the looking-forward-to-grandchildren type, and although she loves Alyssa, I know she wishes I'd done something more with my life. And both of my parents are still furious that I won't tell them who the father of my child is.

How could I, when he doesn't even know?

"Look, Mommy. It's the blue fish movie," Alyssa says, pointing the remote at the TV where she's selected *Finding Nemo*. "I 'member it from when I was little."

I laugh and ruffle her silky hair. "You're still little, munchkin," I tell her.

"Not as little as I used to be."

"That's very true," I say. "And you haven't seen this one in a while. Are you going to watch it tonight?"

"Maybe," she says, drawing the word out. "Or maybe I'll watch *Frozen* again."

That seems likely. *Frozen* is the best movie ever, after all.

The doorbell rings, and I get up to answer it. Tabitha is a few minutes early. When I open the door, she's standing there with a shoebox-sized plastic container and a smile, her laptop bag slung over a shoulder. "I made us cupcakes. Hope you don't mind," she says.

"Oh, you're definitely going to be Alyssa's favorite person tonight." I return the smile and step back to let her in. "Thanks for coming. I'm sorry about the short notice."

Tabitha walks in and waves to Alyssa, who's mugging like mad from the couch. "It's no problem at all," she says. "The only hot date I had tonight was with my bathtub, and that's over now. You look great, Celine."

"Thank you. But I don't have a hot date either," I say with a laugh. "Just a client."

We head to the kitchen, and I grab my purse while Tabitha puts the cupcake box on the counter. She's three years younger than me and runs some kind of online business — I'm not sure exactly what, but she makes decent money and has a super-flexible schedule since she can work

52

anywhere from her laptop. She's also getting dual degrees in programming and business management, attending Oslow and an online school at the same time.

For some reason, she makes me feel old.

Just as I'm about to go back to the living room and say goodnight to my daughter, Tabitha says, "Hey . . . did you hear about Brad Dowling?"

It seems everybody's hearing about Brad lately. Apparently, I can't stop hearing about Brad. "You mean about him waking up?" I say, struggling to keep it casual.

"Yeah. It's wild, right? Five years," she says as she shakes her head. "I can't even imagine what that's like, to wake up and find out you've been asleep that long. He must be pretty strong to survive that. Didn't he get crushed or something?"

"Car accident," I say absently as I wrestle with sudden, painful memories of that night.

Tabitha doesn't seem to notice. She's looking into the distance, a fond smile on her face. "I had such a crush on him in high school," she says. "You know, the whole gorgeous senior, geeky freshman fantasy. I even did that notebook thing, filled a whole one up with his name and mine like we were married. Mrs. Tabitha Dowling, Mr. and Mrs. Brad Dowling, all that dumb stuff, with hearts and flowers all over. God, I was stupid." She shakes herself back to the present and grins. "But I'll bet half the girls who went to Wolfsbrook High that year had a notebook just like it," she says. "Did you know him? You were a junior, right?"

I manage a nod. "We were in college together," I say, and leave it at that. "So, do you need anything else for tonight? I have to head out soon."

"I think we're good. I'll call you if we have any problems."

"Thanks again. I'm just going to say goodbye," I say, already headed for the dining room. "I won't be gone too long, probably eleven at the latest."

"No worries," she calls after me.

By the time I wrap up the mommy's-leaving ritual with Alyssa, Tabitha is in the living room with a plate of cupcakes and two glasses of milk. My daughter hardly notices that I'm going. She's preoccupied with mounds of frosting, not to mention Elsa and Olaf.

I feel worse than ever about Brad. Somehow, I've got to stand up to his mother and tell him what happened, before life carries him away from me again.

* * *

Old City is packed tonight. There's a local band playing live rock music, and they're not half bad, but they sound better from a distance. That's why the three of us are outside, standing by the rail of the concrete barrier that separates the patio from the creek. There's a breeze blowing across the water, still warm for September, and I'm pleasantly buzzed for the second night in a week. It's a record for me.

Jill is decked out in a leather mini-dress and thigh-high boots, sipping her third Jack and Coke as she casually peruses the selection of single males. Unfortunately, there's not much variety — in a town like Wolfsbrook, you find pretty much the same faces every time. And then there's Hannah, with a fire-engine-red silk top over spangled gold tights and her nails painted to match. She's alternately chain-smoking red Marlboros and chewing on her thumbnail as the conversation comes in awkward fits and spurts.

"So," I say after a swallow of my own drink. I'm sticking to tame Tom Collins so I can drive myself home, but Jill took an Uber here. "How does your daughter like kindergarten?"

Hannah startles, and Jill looks on with sly anticipation while she fumbles for an answer and finally says, "She's fine, I think. No complaints."

Well, that's vague. I decide to press a little harder. "Which teacher does she have?"

"Um. Mrs. Somebody," Hannah says with a slight flush. "I'm not sure, actually. I'm terrible with names."

"Is it Mrs. Jocasta?" I say. "Alyssa's in her class."

Hannah bites her lip. "I don't know. Maybe," she says, and looks away. "Can we talk about something else?"

She seems distressed. At this point I'm not sure if she's lying or actually doesn't like to talk about her daughter for some reason, which seems strange, but I'll drop the subject. No reason to alienate her before the closing. "Okay, sure," I say. "What did you do before you came to Wolfsbrook?"

"Oh, you know. Mostly I just hung around being rich," she says with a small laugh. "And I did a little programming for a while. I designed an app. Look, I'll show you." She digs in her purse — Louis Vuitton tonight instead of the Hermès — to come up with a cell phone, and swipes a password to unlock the screen. "Here it is," she says, pointing to an icon. "It's . . . not great or anything, but it works."

The icon is a cartoon megaphone with a funny, wiggly mouth at the wide end and a blue musical note imposed across the center. "Um. What is it?"

Hannah presses her lips together. "It's called ShoutTone," she sort of mutters. "You connect it to your address book, and it uses your conversations and stuff to match celebrity quotes or bits of music to your contacts and give them all unique ringtones and text notification sounds." She gives a one-shouldered shrug. "It works right about half the time."

"That's pretty cool," I say. "Jill's into that kind of programming stuff."

Jill snorts and rolls her eyes. "I made a website once. That doesn't make me a programmer," she says. "It is cool, though. Your app, I mean."

Looking pleased, Hannah starts to say something, but then a female voice shouts across the patio: "Oh my God, Celine! I can't believe you're here!"

It's Missy. Again. I haven't seen her since college, and suddenly she's everywhere I go.

She pushes her way through the crowd toward us, and I notice the blond figure trailing her and realize I never did tell Jill about seeing her the other day. I lean toward her and whisper, "You're not gonna believe this, but Missy's engaged to your nemesis."

She smirks. "Your friend is marrying Angeline Jolie?"

"Not that nemesis," I say. "The one you work with."

Jill's jaw drops as Missy reaches us with her fiancé in tow. "Danny?" she blurts.

Missy's eyes narrow, and the blond looks up and rubs the back of his neck. "It's Dan," he mumbles. "I don't really like Danny."

"Well, you never mentioned that. How was I supposed to know?"

"Excuse me," Missy says with a brittle smile. "You two know each other?"

I step forward and hold out a placating hand. "Jill's a paralegal. She works in Danny — er, Dan's office," I say. "And this is Hannah."

Missy gives Hannah the full side-eye. "Weren't you at Rosalie's funeral?"

Hannah blinks and plucks a fresh cigarette from her pocket. "Yes," she says.

"How did you know her?" Missy demands. "I've never seen you before then, and I know all of Rosalie's friends and family. She was my best friend, you know." Tears form in her eyes. She sniffles and holds a hand out, and Dan fumbles a travel tissue pack out, separates a single tissue and gives it to her.

I don't dare look at Jill's face during this little exchange. If I do, I know I'll burst out laughing.

"She was in my sociology class. In college," Hannah says almost woodenly.

"You went to Oslow?" Missy dabs at her eyes with the tissue. "I didn't see you there."

Hannah shrugs one shoulder. "I was only there for two semesters."

"Well, you . . . oh, God, I sound like such a bitch!" Missy says. She's on the verge of wailing. "I'm sorry. It's just — Celine, you won't believe what happened." She grabs my hand, switching moods from misery to breathless shock. "The police say that the handwriting on Rosalie's suicide note isn't hers. They think she might have been *murdered*," she

56

gushes, and now the tears start falling. "Isn't that horrible? I mean, who would want to kill Rosalie?"

I'm too shocked to respond, but Missy doesn't seem to require a reply. She throws herself into Dan's arms, sobbing. "I'm so sorry. I think I need some air," she says. "It was great to see you again, Celine. Jill, Hannah."

Dan leads her dutifully away, without pointing out that she's already standing outside where there's plenty of air. I stare after them and try to process the news — Rosalie didn't commit suicide. She was murdered. I know Missy tends to exaggerate everything, but she wouldn't lie about this.

And now I have to wonder why whoever faked her suicide would mention Brad.

CHAPTER 10

After Saturday night, the rest of the weekend passes by quietly. I don't even try to tackle the big problems — Brad, the threatening texts, Rosalie's murder, none of it. I just want to get through the closing this afternoon and feel like I've accomplished something. Then I'll worry about the rest.

I go back home for a while after I take Alyssa to school, and wait to head to the office until a little after nine. It's cowardly of me, I know, but I don't want to be alone there with Sabrina. The last text I got is so vague, I'm not sure what it meant, but I know it doesn't rule her out. Though I'm not sure how she would have found out about Joan.

When I walk in, Sabrina and Lucas are at their desks and Maxine is in her office. Courtney hasn't arrived yet, but that's not surprising, since she views her 9 a.m. start time as more of a guideline than a rule. And our fourth agent, Eleanor Finch, rarely comes to the office since she's semi-retired and this job is basically her hobby. Maxine allows it because the two of them went to school together.

Sabrina springs to attention as I'm walking to my desk and gets up to follow me. "Celine, I just wanted to say that I'm really sorry about yesterday," she says in a tone that's about as genuine as a politician during an election year. "I didn't mean it. It was just my time of the month — you know, the old hormones talking."

I manage to glare at her. I'm not sure why she's apologizing, since Lucas didn't see what happened and usually she only backtracks the horrible things she says for show. But maybe Courtney was paying attention after all, and maybe she ratted her out to Maxine.

"Fine, whatever," I say. "Did you . . ."

Send me a text is on the tip of my tongue. I'm determined to say it out loud, to actually confront her, but then I see a small piece of paper on the surface of my desk from a Hughes Real Estate notepad. Written on it, in Maxine's no-frills handwriting, is 'My office, please.'

Dread sinks its claws into my stomach. Something's gone wrong with the sale, I just know it. Did Hannah back out? I thought Saturday night went pretty well, except for Missy's unfortunate interruption. Jill had ended up flirting with some tattooed guy for a while after that, and it was just me and Hannah. She seemed happy when she left. But maybe I'd done something to upset her.

"Is something wrong?" Sabrina says with a tiny smile, and suddenly I know why she apologized. She must've seen Maxine put the note on my desk.

Whatever happened, she knows about it. Because she did it.

"No, not a thing," I force myself to say with a smile, snatching the note to stuff it in my pocket. "But thanks for your concern, Sabrina. I'm sure I'll be fine."

Her smile widens. "I'm not."

I ignore her and walk to Maxine's office on legs that want to tremble. I'm sick with worry, but I think part of it is pure anger. Sabrina's done something to screw this up for me. She must have. And what, exactly, am I going to do about it?

Nothing, a small voice whispers in my head. *Just like you always do.*

God, I hate that I'm so fucking passive.

Maxine's door is ajar. I open it a little more and stick my head in with a nervous smile. She's sitting behind her desk, and she looks up immediately. Her expression is blank.

"You wanted to see me?" I say.

"Yes. Come in." Maxine sighs, and I know it's going to be bad. Even worse when she says, "Close the door."

I do it without looking back where Sabrina and Lucas are sure to be staring at me. She doesn't ask me to take a seat in the chair in front of her desk, but I do anyway. My legs are no longer steady. "What's wrong?" I blurt.

In typical blunt fashion, Maxine gets straight to the point. "Your real estate license is expired," she says. "The commission CC'd me on the email they sent to you. I can't let you close on this property today."

"That's impossible." My head starts throbbing sickly, and my voice is a disbelieving whisper. "It was supposed to be good until next year, but . . . anyway, I renewed it when I got the notification about it expiring. I did it last week, right from my work computer."

Maxine's features soften slightly, and I realize with a shock that she thought I just let it lapse. As if I could be so forgetful, or lazy, about something that important. For an instant I'm furious with her for that. "Well, maybe there was some kind of mix-up at the real estate commission. Crossed wires some-where," she says. "If you can get it straightened out today, fine. But . . . Celine, you know how slow they are at resolving issues."

The anger is building in my gut, a slow burn that sends tremors through me. "And if I can't get it fixed today?"

Her mouth is a firm line. "Then Sabrina will represent the buyer and the agency at the closing today."

"No," I spit out. "I'm not . . . Maxine, I can't lose this sale." My anger comes out as a wheedling plea, and I hate myself for it. "I'll call Hannah. I'm sure she won't mind wait-ing a few days while I sort out—"

"I've already spoken to Ms. Byers," Maxine interrupts. "She doesn't want to wait. And I'm not going to lose this sale for the agency because you allowed your license to lapse."

"I didn't allow it!" My fists clench in my lap. "I told you, I renewed it last week."

Maxine shakes her head. "Not according to the commission," she says. "And you're not going to lose the sale. You'll split it with Sabrina as the agent of record for the seller, once you've straightened out your license."

At once, I'm too furious to speak. *Sabrina.* She's done this, somehow. She couldn't stand the idea of me pulling ahead of her sales record, so she arranged it to make this one even, so she'd still be ahead.

I'm not going to keep my mouth shut this time.

Without another word, I stand, wrench Maxine's door open and stalk out, heading straight for Sabrina's desk. Her cat-ate-the-canary smile turns to a surprised O as she glimpses my face, right before I swat a stack of files off the edge of her desk, scattering manila folders and papers everywhere. "It was you!" I shout, almost delighting in her fear as she cringes back. "You fucked with my license, and you sent those texts."

Sabrina gasps and shoves her chair back, away from me. "I don't know what you're talking about," she stammers.

"Bullshit. I know it was you," I say as I take a step forward. "This is *my* sale. I've worked on it for two years, and you're going to keep your bitchy little hands *out* of it!"

"Celine?" Sabrina says in Maxine's voice. "I said, you won't lose the sale."

I blink rapidly and let out the breath I was holding. I'm still sitting in Maxine's office, my hands clenched in my lap. I never went out there to confront Sabrina. Just like every argument I ever had with my mother, it was all in my head.

I can't do it.

Maxine purses her lips. "Why don't you take the rest of the day off?" she says. "Go home and try to relax, see if you can make any progress with your license. I'll make sure you get your half of the commission, one way or another."

My half. Damn it, it was supposed to be my *whole*. But I can't muster any more anger at the moment, or even a mild disagreement. I'm hollowed out to the core, hurt and humiliated and dazed, unable to think anything beyond *How did this happen? How?*

I know what will happen now. I can see it unfolding. I'll go home with my tail between my legs and say nothing to Sabrina, or anyone else. Eventually I'll get my license straightened out — it'll turn out to be some stupid glitch. Then I'll take fifty percent of my commission and pretend it's great, it's what I wanted all along. It's what I expected.

And I'll carry this hurt around with me forever, like I carry all the others.

CHAPTER 11

When I get home, I finally allow myself to break down and have a good cry, alone in my living room with my face pressed into the couch cushions and my shoes kicked on the floor. I'm crying for Brad, for Rosalie, for my lost commission and the frightening texts, even for Joan Carpenter. And I'm crying for my failure as a human being to have some kind of spine, to stand up for myself. Because there's no one else to stand up for me.

My mother would say that I'm having a pity party and I'm the only one invited. Maybe she's right. But this is the only way I've ever been able to release some of the toxic buildup inside me — even if it's only to make room for more.

An hour later, I'm cleaned up and dressed down, sitting in front of the blank television with my phone in hand. I've spent most of that hour on the phone with the New Hampshire Real Estate Commission, being transferred to various people who had no idea what went wrong but have assured me that they're looking into it and will get back to me within three business days. Of course, I don't have three business days between now and one o'clock this afternoon.

I hate this feeling, the powerless sensation of being an observer in my own life while everything happens around me. I'm going to do something about *something*.

I decide to call Brad.

Retrieving my purse from where I dropped it carelessly on the floor when I came in, I dig around until I find the café receipt with Brad's room and phone number written on it. My hands shake as I tap through to the dial pad. I manage to put in the area code and the first number before I chicken out, swipe back, and redial the main hospital number, where I ask to be connected to the fifth-floor nurse's station.

A woman that might be the same one from before answers on the second ring, and I swallow in an attempt to relieve my dry throat. "Hello," I say. "I was wondering . . . can you tell me whether Brad Dowling has any visitors right now?"

"That's an interesting question. I don't think anyone's ever asked something like that before," the woman says. At least she sounds friendly and not mocking. "I'm honestly not sure if I'm supposed to give out that kind of information. Can I ask why you want to know?"

Because his mother is insane, I want to say. But I don't. "I just really need to talk to him directly," I say. "Without . . ."

"His mother?"

The understanding in this woman's voice lifts a weight from me. "Yes, exactly," I say.

"She's really something else. Don't mention I said that," the woman says.

"Believe me, I won't. Is she there now?"

The woman pauses, and then says, "Unfortunately. She's almost always there."

Disappointment threatens to choke me. I'll never be able to talk to Brad, not while Willa is around. Even if I stand up to her, she simply won't allow it. And I'm not family.

"But I'll tell you this," the woman says quietly. "She never comes in until at least ten, sometimes closer to eleven. And visiting hours start at nine."

A lump forms in my throat, and I feel a sudden kinship with this voice on the phone. "Thank you so much," I say. "Um . . . who are you, if you don't mind my asking? I just really appreciate this."

Another pause. "You won't tell anyone what I said?"

"Never. Trust me, I know how Willa Dowling can get."

She laughs. "I'm Teryn. Teryn Holmes," she says. "I'm a nurse here."

The name sounds very familiar, and I think maybe I went to college with her. "Thank you, Teryn," I say. "I'm Celine Bauman, by the way."

"Oh my gosh. I remember you!" she says with happy surprise. "Weren't you going out with Brad when — oh, no. I'm so sorry," she moans.

"It's okay," I tell her. "But yes. That's why I need to talk to him."

"Wow, yeah, you do. No wonder you're so worried about Willa. That woman is a battleship," she whispers, and then laughs a little. "She actually tried to get me fired, just because I dated Brad for like a month."

I suck in a breath and shake my head ruefully. There is no end to Brad's parade of ex-girlfriends. "That sounds like her," I say. "Well, thank you again. I'll try him tomorrow before the battleship gets there."

Teryn laughs again. "Good luck. I'm rooting for you," she says.

With the call ended, I settle back on the couch and close my eyes. I might be too afraid to confront Willa Dowling, but I'm determined to talk to Brad. And since I'm apparently not going to work for a few days, it's going to happen tomorrow.

Even though I have no idea how to actually tell him something so big, so completely unexpected, after he's already had the shock of learning he was unconscious for five years.

I'm about to get up and go in the kitchen to start some coffee when my front doorbell rings, startling my heart into a higher thump bracket. Whoever it is, it can't be good news. My few friends who might stop by know I'm usually not home during the day, and they have jobs themselves. So maybe it's a salesperson, or a Jehovah's witness . . . or worse, someone *official*.

Everything in me wants to sit here quietly and pretend I'm not here. But when the doorbell rings again, I get up to answer it, driven by the horrible thought that something might've happened to Alyssa.

The front door doesn't have windows or a peephole, so I'll have to open it blind. I steel myself with a deep breath, turn the knob, and pull the door open slowly to find two men in suits standing on my stoop. They're both in their mid-thirties, one with light brown hair and the other with black. They have badges clipped to their belts . . . and guns in holsters. They're police officers, and they have no good reason to be here.

Alyssa.

"What happened?" I gasp, on the verge of fainting. "Oh my God, is my daughter okay?"

The brown-haired one frowns slightly and glances at his partner. "Ma'am, do you have some reason to believe your daughter wouldn't be okay?"

Oh, God. I'm so dizzy. I grab the side of the door and force myself to breathe, squeezing my eyes shut as white flashes behind them. "No. I mean, she's in kindergarten," I blurt. "Did something happen at the school?"

"Maybe we should start over," the brown-haired cop says. "We're not here about your daughter. I'm sorry if I startled you. Are you Celine Bauman?"

The relief that flits through me is short-lived, between the confirmation that Alyssa is safe and this man knowing my name. My stomach is a quivering puddle. I can't even begin to imagine what they want with me — did I get a ticket and forget about it? Can I be arrested for having an expired real estate license?

"Ma'am?" This time the one with black hair speaks. "Could we have your name, please?"

"Yes. I'm Celine Bauman," I finally squeak out. "What . . . what is it?"

They share another glance. "I'm Detective Garfield, and this is Detective Chambers," Brown Hair tells me. "We just want to ask you a few questions. Can we come in?"

Detectives? This isn't right. They have no business being here, and now I'm more angry than scared. In fact, I think that Sabrina is behind this, or maybe Brad's mother. But I'm certainly not going to be railroaded into a false arrest. I have rights.

"No, you can't," I say firmly. "I don't know what this is about, but I haven't done anything. And I don't have to let you in without a warrant. In fact, I suggest that you speak to whoever sent you here again, because they're lying."

Detective Garfield clears his throat. "Ms. Bauman? Can we come in?"

I haven't said any of that aloud. I'm still standing here, staring at them like a deer in headlights. With a mute nod, I step back and pull the door open wider as my stomach churns with self-loathing.

The detectives seat themselves on the couch. In a small act of defiance, I leave the door open and walk slowly to the armchair, settling myself on the edge. "What do you want?"

Detective Chambers takes the lead. "We're looking into the death of Rosalie Phillips," he says as his partner produces a notebook and pen. "You knew her, didn't you?"

"Yes. I mean, I went to school with her," I say. "But . . . it was suicide."

My face heats up as the words leave my mouth, and I'm sure it's turned bright red. I don't know why I said that, after Missy told me that the note was faked and they were investigating it as a murder. I should have just admitted what she said. Now I look like I'm lying to the police.

And they look like they know it.

"We originally thought it was suicide," Chambers says carefully. He has rich brown eyes, and they're digging into me like lasers. "Now we have reason to believe there was foul play involved. But you knew that, didn't you?"

I try to swallow past the lump in my throat. If I change my story now, I'm admitting to lying — but if I keep going, I'll just look more guilty. I have to come clean. "My friend Missy mentioned that they . . . I mean, that you thought the note was a fake, the other night. I just forgot she said that."

They don't seem satisfied by my answer. Garfield scribbles something on his pad, and Chambers leans forward slightly. "That would be Missy Wilson?"

I nod. "Yes. She . . . her and Rosalie were best friends."

"We've already interviewed Ms. Wilson. And that's correct about the suicide note. The handwriting doesn't match Ms. Phillips'," Chambers says, still speaking slowly and searching my face. "Now, Ms. Bauman. I understand that you had a relationship with Bradford Dowling at the time of his accident. Is that correct?"

I still have no idea why they're questioning me, and I'm edging closer to panic with every breath. "What does Brad have to do with—"

"Just answer the question, ma'am," Garfield interjects bluntly.

A fist closes around my stomach. "Yes," I whisper. "I was seeing Brad."

Chambers nods, and Garfield writes something else down. "And what were you doing at Juniper State Park on the afternoon of August 30?"

"What?" I gasp as startled tears form in my eyes. That's the day Rosalie died. And I was nowhere near the park — I was out school shopping with Alyssa all day. "I . . . I wasn't . . . ."

"August 30," Chambers repeats as he takes a folded piece of paper from his pocket and opens it to a computer printout of a Facebook page. From my account. "You logged your location in as Juniper State Park, with friends, at 4:25 p.m.. It's right here. There are photos of the park with the post."

I feel the blood drain from my face as I stare at the paper, almost uncomprehending. This is impossible. "I wasn't. I never," I stammer. "I didn't post that! I was school shopping with my daughter. She started kindergarten this year."

My words sound hollow in my ears. Oh my God, they think I killed Rosalie.

I'm going to throw up.

I desperately swallow bile as Garfield's blue eyes narrow on me. "Are you sure about that?" he says. "We can check the location of your phone when that post was made, you know. We can tell if you're lying."

They can't do that. They *can't*. And even if they could, I'm not lying. I have to get a hold of myself, for Alyssa's sake. She needs me. I can't be her mother from jail.

The thought galvanizes me, and I manage to calm down. "I wasn't there. I was shopping with my daughter," I say again. "That should be easy enough to prove." I rattle off a list of the stores we went to, including the McDonald's we stopped at for lunch. "We got home around 7:30, and I ordered pizza from DiStephano's," I say. "I can probably find most of the receipts."

A laden silence follows my little speech, broken only by Garfield's pen scratching across the paper. Finally, Detective Chambers grunts and stands up, and his partner follows suit. "If you can get us copies of those receipts, we'd appreciate it," he says as he reaches into his pocket again. This time he pulls out a business card and hands it to me. "Ms. Bauman, do you know anyone who'd want to harm Rosalie Phillips?"

"No. No one," I say, shaking my head as I take the card. It's printed with his name and phone number, and the address of the police station. His first name is Oliver. I'm not sure why they're backing off, but I suspect it's because they were bluffing. They can't actually get a location for where my cell phone was over a week ago. And it wouldn't matter if they could, because I didn't do it.

"Well, if you think of anything that might help, please call me. And find those receipts," he says.

Somehow I manage to stand and follow them to the door, and then close it behind them. As the shock wears off, I realize how shattered I feel. I was brought up to trust police officers, to believe they were here to protect and serve. That they actually wanted justice. And I've raised my daughter the same way, to understand that people with badges are friendly. They're supposed to be *safe*. But those two detectives just tried to steamroll me into confessing a crime I didn't commit.

If I hadn't been shopping, if I'd just spent the day at home with my daughter, I am almost certain I'd be in handcuffs right now. They would've arrested me for murder.

I resist the urge to take the business card to the kitchen and burn it on the stove, tucking it into my pocket instead. I'll have to find those receipts — but I'll just deliver them to the station, and I won't call first.

I never want to see Detective Garfield or Detective Chambers again.

CHAPTER 12

I hold it together for longer than I think I'll be able to, faking my way through the rest of the day as I turn the house upside down to find the receipts, drop them off at the police station, and pick up my daughter from school. I pretend so hard that everything is fine, I actually believe it for a while. Through the afternoon, and when Jill comes over for dinner and afterward the three of us hang out and play board games and watch cartoons until Alyssa's bedtime, I'm still okay. I'm fine when I tuck my daughter in and kiss her goodnight.

Then I walk back into the living room and Jill asks me what's wrong, and I fall apart.

I sit on the couch with her, choking back sobs as I tell her everything from the problem with my license to Sabrina stealing my commission, to the horror of the detectives' visit. The awful truth of Rosalie being murdered is really hitting me now, and I can't help but think about the death that *was* my fault. I almost confess that to her, but I can't drag the words out.

When I'm finished, she hugs me tight. "I can't believe those asshole cops," she says in a thick, scraping voice. "I mean, that's insane! Do you want me to tell them I was with you when you were shopping? Because I will."

"No, it's fine. I gave them the receipts." I lean back with a watery smile and swipe at my face. "It was just awful dealing with them. They were so . . . nasty."

"We should sue them," Jill pronounces. "I'm serious. They can't get away with this."

I actually laugh, and it surprises me. "Well, you're the legal expert, but I'm pretty sure you can't sue people for doing their jobs," I say. "Even if they do them badly."

"It'd be for harassment. They shouldn't have come into your house," she says, her eyes blazing with righteous anger. "They need a warrant for that."

A stab of guilt lances me, and I can't bring myself to say that I let them in — or at least, I didn't stop them. "Really, I just want this to be over," I say. "But thank you."

"I didn't do anything. But seriously, I will if you want me to. Just say the word." Jill smirks and flops back against the couch with a sigh. "Do you think somebody really killed your friend?" she says. "That's so crazy. A murder in Wolfsbrook. This place is supposed to be nicer than the city, you know?"

"Yeah, that's what I thought." I lace my hands together to keep them from shaking. My emotions have a tendency to come on fast but take their time leaving, so I'm still feeling a little unsteady. "I don't know, honestly. The police seem pretty convinced."

Jill shakes her head. "Maybe they're wrong."

I'm not so sure about that. If they only suspected the possibility that Rosalie's death wasn't an accident, they wouldn't have pushed me so hard.

Before I can voice my thoughts, my phone vibrates in my pocket. I pull it out and frown at the screen. "It's Hannah," I say. "I'd better take this."

When I answer, she says, "Hi, Celine. It's Hannah Byers." Once again, like I don't know who's calling. Doesn't she understand what caller ID is?

I raise an eyebrow at Jill and say, "Yes, I know. Is everything okay?"

"Well, I have the house keys and I'm moving in," she says. "But you weren't at the office today. What happened?"

My brain stutters and I stand up, pacing away from the couch. She knows what happened. Maxine told her. "Er. I couldn't do the closing, legally," I say. "You told Maxine you didn't want to wait, remember? She must've mentioned my license expiring."

"What? No, I didn't speak to anyone named Maxine," Hannah says. "I went there at one, like you said, and there was this Sabrina woman instead of you. And I asked where you were, and they said you didn't have to be there. But I thought you would be anyway."

"Celine, what is it?" Jill says from behind me.

I wince and wave her off. It's hard to concentrate, because I don't believe what I'm hearing. "Maxine said she called you," I repeat like an idiot, stubbornly clinging to the idea that she couldn't have flat-out lied to me. "There was an issue with my real estate license. I was going to ask if you wanted to wait a few days until I got it sorted out, but Maxine told me she'd already asked, and you wanted to go ahead with today."

Hannah lets out a hearty sigh. "She must have spoken with Julie, then," she says. "I'm so sorry about this, Celine. I didn't know any of it."

My head starts pounding. I almost ask who Julie is, but I decide I'd rather end this call. Whatever happened, it's over now and I'm stuck with a halved commission and a smug bitch of a co-worker. "I'm sorry I couldn't be there," I say. "But I hope you enjoy the house."

I expect to say goodbye and hang up, but Hannah says, "Oh, that's the other reason I called! I'm having a house-warming party on Saturday, and I'd really like you and Jill to come."

A housewarming party at the mansion I got screwed on selling is pretty much the last thing I want to attend, but I'm too polite to refuse her outright. "That sounds interesting," I say. "I might stop by for a few minutes."

"You mean you wouldn't stay?" Hannah sounds crest-fallen, and my conscience twinges.

I bite my lip, and mutter, "Maybe I could stay a while."

"I do hope you will," she says. "It starts at seven. Please come — you and Jill both."

I mumble something about trying and hang up on a heavy breath. "So, what are *you* doing Saturday?" I say as I turn back to Jill with a smirk. "Because Hannah's having a party, and we're invited."

"Oh, boy. That chick is really weird," Jill laughs, and then cocks her head. "Wait, are you actually thinking about going?"

"I don't know." I make my way back to the couch and plop down wearily. "You know me. I'm the queen of not saying no," I sigh. "And I do kind of feel sorry for her. She doesn't seem to have any friends."

Jill flaps a hand dismissively. "Please. She's got plenty of friends," she says. "Lots of Jacksons, Grants and Benjamins. She could buy all the friends she wanted."

It does seem strange that she's rich and friendless. But maybe that's just because there are no other ultra-rich people in Wolfsbrook. Maybe she has friends, but they're scattered, and she goes to visit them in her private jet or something. I have no idea how wealthy people operate.

"Tell you what. If you go, I'll go with you. But I won't have any fun," Jill says, and sticks out her tongue.

A giggle escapes me. "Neither will I, so I'll try not to inflict that on either of us."

"Thank you, dahling. No pish-posh for me," she drawls. "Unless there's a cute pool boy I can pick up."

We both laugh at that. I push Hannah's party out of my head for now and toy with my phone, remembering another call I made that day. The one to the hospital. "I'm going to call Brad tomorrow," I say quietly. "I found out that his mother won't be there until at least ten, so I'll be able to talk to him if I call earlier."

"Oh, honey." Jill flashes me a dismayed look. I'd already told her what happened the first time I tried to call, and she knows I'm more terrified of Willa than ever. In fact, she knows more about me and Brad than anyone else. "Are you sure you want to do that?"

I swallow and nod. "I have to."

"No, you don't," she says in a determined tone. "After the way he treated you that night . . . you don't deserve that. And neither does Alyssa. He never has to know."

The reminder jolts me hard. It *was* an awful argument. But it's not like he hit me, or even threatened me. He just freaked out and left me at the restaurant.

And then nearly killed himself by driving into a concrete barrier wall at forty miles an hour.

"I'm not sure that's fair," I say, trying to be diplomatic. "He was so young, and scared. We both were. I think if it wasn't for the accident, he would've calmed down in a few days, and we could've talked about it rationally. And Alyssa . . . I really should tell him."

Jill purses her lips, and then reaches out to pat my hand. "Maybe don't tell him right away," she says. "Talk to him first, and see if you can feel him out. And if he's still the same old shallow asshole, well . . ." She makes a tipping gesture.

"Yeah. You're probably right," I say, and maybe I won't tell him. Not tomorrow, anyway.

But keeping it from him doesn't *feel* right.

CHAPTER 13

I can't believe I'm doing this, but I'm driving to the hospital. I'm going to talk to Brad in person.

Last night I tossed and turned for hours, agonizing over what to do. I finally decided that calling him would only prolong the inevitable. I need to see him. I *want* to see him.

I never stopped loving him.

We didn't have the perfect relationship, of course, but no one does in college. And it wasn't love at first sight, either. We'd been friends since the beginning, nothing more, and I watched him go through girlfriend after girlfriend with a kind of bemused disbelief that anyone could have enough strength to be with that many girls, let alone go through the fallouts when he inevitably broke it off. But he was upfront with everyone about not looking for a commitment. Flings only for Brad Dowling the Football King.

That's why I stayed on the sidelines for so long. That's why I told him about Joan, and she ended up dead.

But then one night, a bunch of us were at Monkey Shines — a super-popular college bar just off campus — and Brad asked me to come outside with him for a minute. So I went, not thinking much of anything about it. Until he kissed me.

"What was that for?" I'd asked him.

He'd shrugged, and looked at me with those deep green eyes that had charmed the panties off dozens of co-eds. The same eyes I still see every time I look at my daughter.

"I've never kissed you before," he'd said. "I just wanted to see what it was like."

"Well . . . what was it like?"

He'd smiled. "Amazing," he said, and kissed me again.

That time, I'd kissed him back. And I went to his frat house room with him, knowing I'd fallen under his spell, not caring, even though I knew I'd care in the morning. I stayed all night. When I woke up, I was prepared to do the walk of shame back to the dorms and endure the teasing.

But he woke up too, and asked me to stay for breakfast. Then he held my hand and walked me over to the dorms while everyone stared at us. And he asked for a proper date that night, just him and me.

I spent an entire year with him, the whole time thinking I had to be dreaming. But it wasn't a dream — it was a nightmare waiting to begin, when I asked him about our future together and he flipped out, stormed away and ended up might-as-well-be-dead.

I didn't know I was pregnant until a week after the accident, when it was far too late to tell him.

Hayhurst Memorial Hospital looms into view, a spangling-clean modern structure of blue glass and white cement. This place is actually the premiere regional trauma center in the northeast, despite its location in humble little Wolfsbrook. I have no doubt that if there was a better hospital within five hundred miles of here, Mr. and Mrs. Dowling would've whisked Brad away from this town without looking back. He definitely would've been out of my life forever then, and at the moment I'm still not sure whether that would have been better. But I'm about to find out.

I follow the signs to the hospital parking garage, ease my car into one of the too-narrow parking spots, and try to remember where I parked as I follow more signs to an elevator, across an elevated, glassed-in walkway and into the hospital. There's no desk or reception area here, just a lot of hallways and closed doors, so I hunt around for an elevator and ride to the fifth floor.

It's just after nine when I walk into a brightly lit corridor and spot a desk with a sign that reads NURSE'S STATION. There are two women in scrubs behind the desk, one who's forty-something and looks irritated with the world, and the other about my age who's just familiar enough to make me smile as I approach.

I haven't seen her in years, but I recognize Teryn.

She catches sight of me, and her face lights up as she skirts around the desk. "Celine, you made it!" she calls, reaching out for a hug. I'm glad to hug her back. Familiar faces are hard to come by in a hospital. "You should have plenty of time before the battleship docks," she says under her breath, snorting laughter. "Do you know which room he's in?"

I nod. "548, right?" I say, as if I haven't held that number in my mind since the moment the receptionist gave it to me.

"That's the one. Turn left at the end of this hall, and it's the third room on the right," she says, pointing past the nurse's station. "You know, I think he's going to be very glad to see you."

"I hope so," I say, and then bite my lip. "Is he . . . really messed up?"

Teryn smiles. "Considering what he's been through, he's in amazing shape," she says. "He's already taking a few steps every day. Dr. Salinas — that's his doctor — calls him a blue-eyed miracle. I guess it's supposed to be a joke, because of his green eyes. But nobody thinks it's very funny," she adds with a wink.

Well, at least there's some good news. She doesn't mention brain damage, so I'm hoping that means there isn't any. "Thank you," I say. "I'd better get down there, before the HMS Willa steams in."

"Good idea," Teryn laughs. "Hey, stop by on your way out. Maybe we can grab a cup of coffee and catch up for a few minutes."

"Sounds good to me."

My resolve almost fails me as I walk down the hall. The closer I get to the left turn that will take me to Brad, the harder my heart beats, until I'm sure it's going to explode. At least I'm in a hospital, so they can save me if I have a heart attack.

Soon enough, I find room 548. The door is open just enough to peek inside, giving a glimpse of white walls and part of a window. I'm not sure whether I should knock. Maybe I should just walk in, since it's open. But as I reach for the door, I think maybe he's sleeping. He could be trying to get some rest while his mother isn't here to harangue him.

I finally realize that I'm making excuses to keep from facing this. I let out a long breath and push the door open.

The room is good-sized, but there's only one bed, and Brad is in it. His eyes are closed. That's all I notice as I step inside carefully, looking around at everything but him before I have to really see him, because I know how much that's going to hurt.

There's a large, room-length window on the far side, and the wide windowsill is completely covered with flowers, cards, balloons and stuffed animals. A big-screen TV is mounted on the wall opposite the foot of the bed. Under the television and slightly off to the side, there's a brown door that probably leads to a bathroom. There are monitors, IV stands, a blood pressure machine, a privacy curtain, a folded wheelchair in a corner. The normal trappings of a hospital.

And there is Brad.

When I focus on him, all the breath leaks out of me in slow motion. I have awful, vivid memories of him after the accident — his face a pulpy mass of blood and bruises and black stitches with a thick plastic tube shoved down his throat, both arms and one leg in stiff white casts with every protruding finger and toe swollen and purple-black. The way his chest jerked up suddenly with every hiss of the mechanical ventilator and went down gradually, like a deflating balloon.

But now the stitches are out, the casts are off, the blood and bruises are gone. He's slimmed down but not gaunt

— probably because he was so muscled before the accident. Both eyes are marked with dark half-circles of exhaustion, and his lips are dry and cracked, the color of them too dark. There's a sheet pulled to his waist, and his arms rest on top of it with IV needles taped to the backs of his hands and a large bruise on his upper arm. A small, bloody blister rests at the center of the bruise like a bullseye.

My throat wrenches shut. I can't believe I'm looking at him, breathing on his own. Alive. It's the moment I never dared to dream of — and I still don't know what to say.

I take a tentative step toward him, and he shifts slightly. "I already choked down breakfast," he says without opening his eyes, in a voice that sounds like sandpaper and nails scratching on wood. He tries to smile. "It's not bath time, is it?"

"Brad," I whisper. "Oh, my God . . ."

His eyes snap open. They're slightly bloodshot, but still the same brilliant green I remember as they focus on me and widen in surprise. "Celine?" he rasps.

I nod like crazy and stumble the rest of the way to the bedside, barely noticing the tears that start to slip down my face. I can't bring myself to touch him, or even to look at him directly, so I stare at the shapes of his legs under the sheet. "I'm so sorry," I say in trembling tones. "So sorry."

Something warm and dry caresses my arm, and I realize it's him. He slides a palm down my forearm, takes my hand in his and squeezes gently. "Why are *you* sorry?" he says. "It was my own damned stupid fault."

A single sob wrenches from my throat, and I clap my free hand over my mouth. I won't break down in front of him, not here. He's probably had more than enough people crying over him.

"Please, sit down," Brad says. I finally look at his face, and he's smiling. "Unless you're not staying? I wouldn't blame you if you don't. I know you called the other day, and my mother . . ." A dark cloud passes over his expression.

"I'd like to stay. If you don't mind," I say.

"Of course I don't. That's why I asked you to sit."

The teasing note in his awful, strained voice sounds like the old Brad, and I almost start bawling again. But I hold it back and take a seat in the big stuffed chair next to the bed. "I hardly know what to say," I admit softly. "Everything I can think of sounds so trite."

"Just don't tell me what a miracle I am, and we're good," he says. "So . . . what have you been up to for the past five years? I've just been lying around."

I gasp in a thick, wet breath, and my eyes sting with tears.

"I'm sorry. That was a bad joke." Brad reaches through the bars of the bed rail, and I take his hand when it falls short. "I'm trying to laugh my way through this, you know? Five years. Jesus." His eyes close briefly. "They say laughter is the best medicine."

"And how's that working out for you?" I say dryly.

He actually laughs, deep and genuine, and I can't help laughing with him. "Not so great," he says. "I happen to think morphine is the best medicine. I've got this happy button, see?" He lifts a white cord near his other hand with a plastic bulge in the middle, sporting a single blue button. "Every time I press this, I get really happy."

I smirk. "You must be pressing the shit out of that button when your mother is around, then."

He whoops in a breath and wheezes it out. "Oh, God, that hurts," he gasps with a smile on his face, waving a hand when my face falls in dismay. "Hurts so good, I mean. I think this is the first time I've really laughed since I woke up."

At least I can smile knowing I've made him happy for a minute. "I'm glad you can still laugh," I say.

"Celine." He stares at me, shakes his head slightly. "This is just so . . . bizarre. I mean, to me, the last time I saw you was a week ago. I actually woke up and wondered why you weren't here, if you were really so mad at me that you wouldn't come to see me in the hospital. I remembered knowing I was going to crash, that it was going to be really bad, and then . . ." A shuddering breath leaves him. "Five years," he whispers. "God, I was so *stupid*."

"No, you weren't. It was an accident," I say firmly. "You can't blame yourself for that."

"Can't I?" He scowls furiously at the ceiling. "I was drunk, Celine. Very, very drunk. My blood alcohol level tested at almost three times the legal limit when they brought me in after the crash. The only reason I'm not recovering in prison right now is that no one else was involved, and the DA figured that sixteen broken bones and five years in a coma was punishment enough. Plus, my folks probably paid him off."

I'm too shocked to respond. Three times the legal limit? He had one, maybe two glasses of wine that night.

"I know I didn't drink much there," he says, as if he's reading my mind. "But when I left, I hit the liquor store. And then . . ." He trails off and winces. "Let's just say I compounded the huge mistake I made when I left you in the first place."

Mistake? "You mean . . . you would've come back to me?"

"Yes. God, yes," he breathes. "It's all I've wanted since the minute I woke up. To go back to that night, apologize for making such an ass of myself. And beg you to forgive me."

"Oh, Brad. I—"

"Get away from my son, you little *slut*!"

The drillbit shriek of Willa Dowling's voice floods the room, and Brad and I both jump like a couple of kids caught making out in the back of a car. I shoot to my feet and let go of his hand, cringing from his mother's advance.

"Mother, stop it!" Brad cries hoarsely. "I told you, it wasn't Celine's fault. She had nothing to do with the accident."

Willa freezes in the center of the room, panting like a bull. Her green eyes, much paler than her son's, are bulging marbles that show far too much white. Her face is patched with hectic, ruddy spots beneath her makeup, and her dark gray-streaked hair sticks out in flyaways from a hastily formed bun.

82

"I don't care. I want her out of this room." Spittle flies from her lips as she speaks.

"It's *my* room, Mother. And I want her to stay."

"No, it's okay. I'll go," I say quickly, reaching down to take Brad's hand one more time. "But I'll come back and visit you again, if that's okay with you."

It takes a lot for me to say that while Willa's glare burns a hole in my back, and I'm almost proud of myself. Okay, it's not exactly standing up to her. But it's a start.

"I'd like that," Brad says. "Hold on, though. I want to . . ." His whole body tenses, and he starts to sit up.

"Bradford! You need your rest," his mother quavers. "You shouldn't move around—"

"Mother, will you *please* stop talking for one lousy minute," he growls with concentrated effort. "I love you, but you're making me nuts here."

The real miracle is that Willa actually shuts up.

"Do you want some help?" I say tentatively.

He shakes his head, grimacing as he grabs the bed rail. "I have to practice doing this myself," he says through clenched teeth — not angry, but determined. "I refuse to stay in this bed one minute longer than I have to."

Though I've never been in a coma for five years, I completely understand that.

Finally he's sitting up fully, panting a little. He pauses for a minute, and then lowers the bed rail and eases his legs over the side, so he's facing me.

He opens his arms, and a tremulous smile lifts his lips. "Can I have a hug?" he says.

It's almost impossible to resist falling into his arms immediately. But he's so frail, so weakened, that I'm afraid I'll knock him back down. I take it easy, stepping up close and wrapping my own arms tenderly around his chest.

His breath hitches as he enfolds me with surprising strength. "I promise I won't break," he murmurs. "Celine, just . . ."

I take the hint and squeeze, pressing against his body. He's still so firm, so solid and real and *alive*. A shiver runs down my spine, and I draw back just enough to kiss his dry cheek. "I forgave you five years ago, the minute you walked out," I whisper.

He stares at me. "Really?"

"Really," I say, and plant another kiss on his forehead. "I'll see you again, soon."

His wondrous smile bolsters me as I turn and walk past Willa-zilla, who's still glaring daggers at me. I step from the room and into the hallway, feeling lighter than I have in days. And I make it about ten steps down the corridor before I freeze in horror.

Did that actually happen? Or did I just imagine it?

Oh, God, I can't remember.

Did I really ignore Willa's screaming demands and stay, and watch Brad not only defend me, but go through all that effort just to hug me? Or did I lock up when she started screaming and stand there imagining everything that came after, before I bolted from the room without another word?

It feels like it really happened, that things actually went well despite Willa's interruption, but I just can't be sure. And I can't bring myself to go back into that room to find out.

My cheeks burn with shame, and I rush back down the corridors toward the elevators, shielding myself with a hand as I pass the nurse's station. If Teryn is still there, I can't face her. The elevator takes about a million years to arrive on the floor, and I stumble inside and push the button for the parking garage level, shoving myself into a corner as far from the two other passengers in the elevator as possible.

Somehow I blunder to my car and get in. My eyes are already streaming when I shut the door behind me, and within seconds I'm weeping with my forehead pressed to the steering wheel and my hands over my face. I can't deal with this. I don't know *how* to deal with this.

The next time I come to see Brad — which I'm determined to do, in spite of the disaster this has become — I'll have to go through this all over again.

I'm not sure how long it's been when I finally calm down and trail off into hitching, uneven breaths. I rummage around in my console for a napkin to wipe my face, and then blow my nose and crumple the napkin into a cup holder. I'll wait a few more minutes before I try to drive, since I'm still shaking.

Just then, my phone chimes.

I almost don't want to look. But I pull the phone from my pocket and unlock the screen to find I have a new text. For some reason I'm not shocked to see the message from the mystery number, bold as brass at the end of the thread.

How dare you speak to him? You don't deserve him!

Instinctively, I decide that it must be Willa sending the texts. But I think about it for a moment and realize that's not necessarily true. It *could* be Willa. But it could also be literally any of Brad's dozens of exes, from high school or college.

The only thing I know for sure is that whoever it is, they're watching me somehow. They're watching me very closely.

And they won't stay back and watch forever.

CHAPTER 14

It takes me longer than I want to calm down after the latest text. I don't reply this time, because I can't bear even one more cutting or frightening remark. Finally I get myself together, start the car and drive out of the parking garage, heading for the grocery store in my neighborhood. I just want to pick up a few essentials and go home. Maybe I'll even take a nap before it's time to get Alyssa from school.

I'm zoned out on the drive to the store and weighed down while I park and trudge inside to grab a cart. Once I get through the automatic doors and into the big, cool produce section, I shake myself and take a few deep breaths to shed the remaining stress. Nothing's wrong with me. Not one thing. I'm just a happy suburban mom on a perfectly normal day, with a dead boyfriend who's come back to life and an unknown crazy person who may or may not be threatening me.

Everything is just fine.

I head slowly into the rows of colorful produce, thinking about a nice salad. I'll make spaghetti for dinner tonight, one of Alyssa's favorites, with a salad and some garlic bread. But I won't settle for a bag of pre-mixed salad. I'll make it fresh, with two kinds of lettuce and lots of crunchy vegetables. Alyssa loves helping me make salad.

I've got iceberg and romaine lettuce and a bag of carrots in my cart, and I'm picking through the loose green peppers when from the corner of my eye I notice someone pushing a cart toward me. They're coming deliberately, like they mean to talk to me.

Though I don't make eye contact, I know who it is before she speaks.

"Hi, Celine," Hannah says as she stops in front of the cucumbers. "I'm so glad you shop here. I was wondering if this was a good store."

I almost tell her that I only shop here because it's close to my house, and there's another store a lot closer to hers. But I grit my teeth into a smile instead and look over at her. "It's not bad," I say. "They have good sales here, sometimes."

Hannah starts to say something, but then changes her mind. Probably something along the lines of not having to worry about things being on sale. Instead she says, "Did you get your real estate license fixed?"

"No, not yet." Even as I answer, I wonder why I'm encouraging this conversation. "It's all a big bureaucracy, you know? Once something gets screwed up, it takes forever to fix."

Hannah nods in sympathy, as if someone who pays four hundred thousand dollars in cash for a house so they don't have to bother with 'mortgage stuff' could understand the struggles of dealing with bureaucracy. "Do you handle your license online, like the DMV?" she says. "That's probably the reason there's still a problem. Everything is electronic these days, and it's so easy for things to get botched up."

"Mm-hm." I'm barely listening as I slip two green peppers in a plastic bag and wish she'd go away. I've got a pity party waiting for me at home, and she's not invited. "I guess that's the way it goes."

"Yes, it's really insane," she says, foiling my attempts to shake her as I move toward the fancy dressings, and she follows me like a lost puppy. "You wouldn't believe how easy it is to manipulate electronic data, or to access other people's information. I mean, take my app. I barely know

87

anything about programming, but it can pull data from anyone's Facebook page and use it, or even post on their page."

I stop, and my hands clench around the bar of the shopping cart. "What was that, about posting on people's Facebook?"

"My app can do that," she says, looking at me strangely. "And I'm not good at programming or anything. All I did was watch a few online tutorials, and presto, I'm an app developer. Are you okay, Celine?"

I'm not sure I am. I never tried to figure out how that post about checking in at Juniper State Park got on my page. At the time, I was too terrified of the detectives to think straight. But now I'm wondering whether someone posted it deliberately. And the only reason I can think for anyone to do that is ridiculous, straight out of a movie.

They're trying to frame me for Rosalie's murder.

"I'm fine," I say out loud, banishing the thought even as my mind tries to somehow connect it with the threatening texts. If I let myself start thinking crazy like that, I'll never stop. "Listen, I'm still going to try and make it to your party."

I say that hoping Hannah will be satisfied and go elsewhere to continue her shopping, which she hasn't even started yet, judging by her empty cart. But it only makes her more eager to talk. "It's going to be fun," she assures me. "I'm having it catered, and I'm thinking about hiring a deejay. Or a live band. Which do you think is better? Oh, and bring a bathing suit, because the pool will be open."

"That sounds great," I mutter weakly, wondering if she actually expects me to answer the deejay-live band conundrum. "I'd go with the deejay," I add, in case she does.

"Really? Hmm, maybe you're right. At least that way the music is guaranteed to be decent," she says. "What kind of music do you like?"

Okay. I really don't want to be BFFs with this woman. "All kinds," I say as dismissively as I can manage, angling my cart for an escape. "But you should use whatever kind of music you want. It's your party."

See you later is on the tip of my tongue as I start away from her, but she drags her cart around and starts talking again. "I think your job is really interesting," she says. "How do you become a real estate agent? Is it hard?"

I'm not sure if she's mocking me or trying to flatter me. Either way, this is not a conversation I want to have. "It's not that hard," I say. "If you really want to know, you can ask Maxine Hughes. She's always happy to hear from people who want to be agents."

"Maybe I'll do that," she says, and I'm inwardly relieved. Generally, people ask about your career to be polite — and even if they say they want to do the same thing, they never follow through. "Well, I'd better run. The movers are coming soon with another load, and if I'm not there to direct them, it'll be a disaster. See you later, Celine."

"Bye, Hannah."

At least I didn't have to extricate myself from that. If Hannah's really going to shop here often, I might consider looking for another grocery store to frequent.

I grab the rest of what I need quickly, looking down aisles before I enter them to make sure I don't bump into Hannah again, and then check out and head home. The visit with Brad this morning already seems like a distant memory that I don't have to dwell on. Though I know I can't dismiss him from my life again, I feel better convincing myself that there's no need to deal with all the complications that surround him right this minute.

After I get to the house and put the groceries away, I decide to take a nice, long bath instead of a nap. That's something I haven't done in quite a while. I head to my bedroom, strip and put on a soft robe, and I'm hunting through my closet for comfortable clothes when my phone rings from the bed where I tossed it.

For some reason I think it's Hannah. I escaped her, and she's still bothering me. But the name on the screen is Maxine Hughes.

"Hello?" My heart is already sinking as I answer the call. It's probably more bad news. Maybe the technical issues with my real estate license are permanent. Maybe I'm fired. Maybe Sabrina ran off to Vegas with all the money, including my half.

"Celine, I'm glad I caught you," Maxine says. "Did you get the message from the commission?"

Great. It's about my license. "No, I didn't," I say. "What's wrong now?"

"Nothing, actually. They found the problem and fixed it, so you're all set. Your license is valid."

I want to be happy about that. But I can't quite get there. A one-day-resolution is fast for the real estate commission, but it's still one day too late. "Okay. Thank you," I say, wondering why they didn't call me. They must have emailed. I haven't checked my work email since yesterday morning. "Maxine, I was thinking about—"

"You'll be here tomorrow, won't you?" Maxine says, interrupting me just before *taking a few days off* comes out of my mouth. "We had an inquiry from a new seller with a very high-end property, and I told them about your success with the Quintaine home. They want to sign on with you, and they're highly motivated to sell."

This is Maxine's backhanded way of apologizing for giving my commission to Sabrina. She's trying to bulldoze me into gratitude. Even though I did want a few days off, I'll take the client — but I'm going to be petty and not actually thank her for it. "All right. I'll be there in the morning," I say. "See you then."

I hang up before she can say anything further and toss the phone back on the bed. My tiny flash of defiance feels good for a minute, and when the guilt and self-recrimination for being rude hits me, I try to ignore it.

My ignorance doesn't last long, but it's nice while it does.

CHAPTER 15

Alyssa has her first show-and-tell today at school. She wanted to take a spaghetti dinner in to share with the class, but I managed to convince her that it was a better idea to bring something non-edible. She decided on her pinecone collection from our many mini-vacations with Jill to the cabin, which she's been gathering since she was two.

Now she's safely in class with her pinecones, and I'm pulling into the office, once again arriving a little after nine. It's another small act of defiance, not coming in early, and I doubt Maxine will notice. But it makes me smile.

Unfortunately, my private smile withers when I walk inside to Maxine emerging from her office, with Hannah Byers right behind her.

I don't get the chance to ask what she's doing here. Hannah rushes over to me, grinning broadly, and says, "I asked Maxine about being a real estate agent, just like you said. And I'm going for it!"

"Going for what?" I stammer, shooting a quick frown at Maxine.

"Hannah's going to join our agency," Maxine says. "I've just helped her enroll in an online licensing course, and she's going to start sitting in today, learning the ropes."

I blink and look around the office, as if this is some practical joke and I'll find hidden cameras somewhere recording my reaction. But all I see is a new desktop computer on the formerly empty desk next to mine. None of the other agents are here, so if she's supposed to be sitting in today . . .

"I'm so excited that I'll get to work with you," Hannah says.

Good God, what is it with this woman? I really don't understand why she's latched onto me so hard. First she has a daughter just like mine, and now she wants a job just like mine? This is getting a little ridiculous.

"It's a great opportunity," Maxine says, looking pleased with herself. "Since you're just getting started with new sellers, Hannah will be able to see the whole process from step one. She'll be ready to jump in right away once she completes her license."

Yes, a great opportunity. For Hannah. Not so much for me, because if I'm supposed to babysit her while she takes the licensing course, I'll have to be in the office more often. And coordinate my schedule more carefully. And spend more time with Hannah.

None of these are things I want to do.

"Why don't you give her to Sabrina, like you did with my commission?" I say. "She doesn't have a child to take care of, and she's really good at kissing ass when there's something in it for her."

Except I don't actually say that. What I do is grin and bear it, like always.

I make the appropriate congratulatory small talk and head to my desk, half hoping that Hannah changes her mind and leaves. But she follows me, sits down at the newly equipped desk, and stares at me while I start up my computer and go through my briefcase.

I decide that if I'm going to be working with her, I'd like a few more answers.

"So, did you ever remember the teacher's name for your daughter's class?" I say casually. "I'm still trying to figure out if she's in the same class as Alyssa."

Hannah sighs. "I'm really not good with that sort of thing," she says.

I can't imagine not knowing who my child's teacher is, but maybe it's not that weird. I admit, I can be a little anal about things that involve my daughter. "You said her birthday is in October, right? What day?"

"The twenty-first," she says promptly.

At least she pulled that one out fast, and it's not the same as Alyssa's. But it is the same numbers reversed, because Alyssa's is the twelfth.

I remember that last time she asked not to talk about her daughter, so I switch gears. "Didn't you say that you went to Oslow State for a while?" I ask her. "I went there too, but I never graduated. I . . . got pregnant and dropped out." I almost mention Brad and the accident, but I really don't want to discuss that with her. I don't even talk to my actual friends much about that, except Jill.

Hannah brightens a bit. "We have so much in common. That's exactly what happened to me," she says. "We must've been there for the same years, since our daughters were born so close together. I don't think I ever had a class with you, though." She smiles. "I would've remembered."

"So we're the same age, too," I say. "Did you grow up in Wolfsbrook?"

If she says yes, I'll know she's lying about that. She would've been in my graduating class, and I remember just about everyone I went to high school with.

But she shakes her head. "I came here from Oslow," she says vaguely.

I notice that she doesn't say that's where she grew up.

My suspicions about her are elevated, but I don't feel all that confident interrogating people. In fact, my pulse is already starting to race. I drop the questions and instead start introducing her to the websites and programs she'll be using, since she's randomly decided to be a real estate agent. She seems to pay attention and take an interest. At least that's something, if I'm going to be stuck with her.

But I've already decided to find out more about Hannah on my own, and I know where to start looking.

CHAPTER 16

That night as I'm tucking Alyssa into bed, she says, "Mommy, if you call my school and ask them, will they put Izzy in my class?"

I smile at her. "Probably not, munchkin," I say. "Is she having problems with her class, or do you two just want to spend more time together?"

"Well, yes. She's my best friend," Alyssa says with an unspoken *duh*, as if I've just asked the dumbest question in the world. "But Izzy doesn't like her teacher. Mrs. Jocasta is nicer than Miss Wilson, so she wants to be in my class."

"I see. In that case, Izzy's mommy would have to ask the school if she can be in a different class."

"Oh." My daughter sighs. "What if it's not Izzy's real mommy?"

Oh, boy. I should've realized that when she started school, Alyssa was going to be a little more exposed to different types of families. She'd have a lot of questions about them. And I knew that eventually, it would lead to questions about her father. She's only asked about her father once, when she was three, and I told her that he lived somewhere else. That had satisfied her then, but it wasn't likely to the next time she asked.

I am going to have to tell Brad about her, very soon.

"Whoever takes care of Izzy all the time is the person who should call the school," I finally tell my daughter. "Whether it's her real mommy or not."

I wait for her to ask about stepmothers, or adoption, or some other type of non-traditional arrangement. But she says, "Oh, good, because Izzy's real mommy doesn't like her. So she wouldn't call my school."

My heart goes out to Alyssa's friend, even though I've never met her. No child should believe that her mother doesn't like her — a feeling I understand through personal experience. That's one of the reasons I try so hard, maybe too hard, to make sure my daughter never feels that way.

"Well, *Alyssa's* mommy loves her very much," I say, leaning down to kiss her.

She giggles. "Alyssa loves her mommy very much, too."

"I'm glad to hear it. Goodnight, sweetheart," I say. "Sweet dreams."

"Goodnight, Mommy."

She snuggles into her covers, and I turn off the light and leave the door half-open as I head for the third bedroom, which I've made a home office. Since Hannah won't tell me anything about her history, I've decided to find out what I can for myself.

I sit down at the desk and open Facebook first, typing 'Hannah Byers' into the search bar. It returns almost a hundred People results. I scroll down the list, looking at profile photos and opening separate pages for accounts that don't have pictures of people, but none of them seems to be her.

Okay, so she doesn't have a Facebook page, but she developed an app that uses Facebook. That's not weird or anything.

Who am I kidding? Everything about Hannah is weird.

I switch to Google and enter her name. Most of the top results are lists of social media profiles and a few items about someone who works at a museum, which isn't her. I add 'New Hampshire' to the search and run it again.

This time I get results. The first is a news article from the *Nashau Telegraph* with a stark, ominous headline: *CEO OF BYERS FINANCIAL DIES IN DEADLY RESIDENTIAL BLAZE.*

I click through to the article and read the brief text with mounting horror.

Last night, a fire claimed the lives of Byers Financial CEO Jonathan Byers and his wife, Elizabeth Byers, in the largest residential blaze Nashau has seen in fifty years. The Byers' 25-room mansion, situated at the top of Birch Hill, was fully engaged at the time firefighters arrived on the scene, and the home was deemed a total loss. Investigators believe that arson may have been involved and are launching a detailed inquiry into the fire.

The couple's adult daughter, 24-year-old Hannah Byers, was home at the time but survived the fire. Circumstances surrounding Ms. Byers' escape from the deadly blaze are unclear at this time, as the young woman suffered a break-down at the scene and was taken to St. Joseph's Hospital for treatment.

Mr. Byers was the founder and CEO of Byers Financial, a hedge fund management company with reported annual rev-enues of $500 million. Mr. Byers' personal worth has been reported as high as one billion dollars, and he frequently appeared on the Forbes 400 list. Mrs. Byers was a home-maker and advocate for various charities, including Habitat for Humanities and the Bumblebee Conservation Trust.

As the couple's only child, 24-year-old Hannah stands to inherit the bulk of the Byers fortune. At the time of this writing, Ms. Byers was not available for comment.

I get to the end of the article and shiver. Beyond the shock of finding out Hannah's parents died in a fire that might have been deliberately set, I also learn that she's orig-inally from Nashau, like Brad. And the date of the article places the fire at about a week after Brad's accident.

Of course, that doesn't have to mean anything. Nashau is a big city. But lately I've been getting a lot more suspicious about coincidences.

I return to the results page and find another article further down, this one from a newspaper called the *Horizon*. And it's apparently all about Hannah, because the title is *Byers Heiress Committed to Psychiatric Hospital*.

The article is longer than the first one, but it doesn't go into much personal detail. It says that due to 'mental strain resulting from the traumatic events leading to the death of her parents,' Hannah had developed several psychological disorders and had been involuntarily committed to the Seton-Frischer Clinic, an isolated 'mental retreat' in the White Mountains.

It also refers to her committal as a 'sentence' of five years. Which suggests that she came to Wolfsbrook right after she was released, bought a house worth nearly half a million dollars, and decided to become a real estate agent.

There's no mention of a daughter, anywhere. But if she does actually have a child, she was pregnant when she was committed and gave birth while she was at the clinic.

I don't know much about psychiatric hospitals, but I'm pretty sure they wouldn't let involuntarily committed patients raise children.

Though I'm not sure I want to find out any more about Hannah Byers, I return to the search results and look through them. There isn't much more to read. Another brief article from the *Telegraph* reports that the Byers mansion fire was ruled arson, but police and investigators were unable to identify the culprit. I find Hannah's name mentioned on a Facebook page for a Nashau high school, one in a list of her graduating class. And then once more, in an article about Oslow State football team's big win over UMass. I actually remember that game from my freshman year at college.

Hannah's name is in the caption of a crowd photo taken at the front row of the game, but it's not the only one I recognize.

She's standing next to Joan Carpenter.

I close the browser with a hand that's starting to shake and sit there staring at the computer screen for a long time. There are too many coincidences here to ignore. I have no idea why, but Hannah is in Wolfsbrook — and in my life — for a reason. And I suspect it's connected to Brad.

Tomorrow morning, I'm going to see him again.

CHAPTER 17

I head out to Hayhurst right after I bring Alyssa to school, arriving firmly in the Willa-less window of time. Teryn isn't at the nurses' station today, and all of the staff seems strangely subdued. But at least Brad seems happy to see me.

Hopefully, that means I didn't imagine what happened the last time I was here.

He's sitting in the wheelchair this morning instead of the bed, and he wheels toward me and stands for a hug. That convinces me the other day wasn't my imagination. We hold each other a little longer this time, and it feels so good that I want to cry.

"I'm sorry. I know you're tired of hearing it, but I have to say that you really are in amazing shape," I say as I let go reluctantly.

He settles back in the chair with a sigh. "Yeah, I guess. My parents made sure I had the best coma therapy that money can buy." His smile is bitter, and I'm not sure whether it's directed at the coma, or his parents. "Please, come in and sit down."

I follow him to the chair by the bed. As I take a seat, he says, "I'm glad you decided to come back, after my mother's outburst. I really hate the way she gets sometimes."

I shrug and smile. "Well, I didn't come to see your mother."

The way he looks at me stirs up things I haven't felt in years, and I have to glance away.

"So," he says after a slightly awkward pause. "Did you hear about Teryn Holmes?"

I'm not sure how, but suddenly I know that something terrible happened to her. Cold shivers down my back and tightens my skin as I say, "What about her?"

Brad shakes his head slowly. "She died. Right here at the hospital," he says.

"Oh, no!" I blurt, completely shocked in spite of my premonition, or whatever it was. She's *dead*, just like that? It doesn't seem possible. "How? What happened? I saw her Tuesday morning when I came to visit, and she . . . well, she seemed fine."

My voice starts to thicken as the guilt sets in. She'd asked me to have coffee with her, and I couldn't be bothered because I was too scared of Willa. And now we'll never be able to catch up. God, I'm such a pathetic piece of shit.

"They're not sure how yet, but it actually happened the day you were here. Tuesday," Brad says. "I guess they found her on a couch in the staffroom. She'd been dead for hours by the time they figured it out, because everyone thought she was sleeping and left her alone. It was pretty awful."

I let out a soft groan. For the moment, I can't form words. It *is* awful . . . and she was so young, just like Rosalie.

Oh, God. She had something else in common with Rosalie, too.

"You should be careful, Celine," Brad says in a tone that tries and fails to be light. I can hear the misery, and maybe even fear, below the surface. "My exes are dropping like flies. First Rosalie, and now Teryn."

It's almost exactly what I just thought, and it startles me rigid. The warning that was meant to be playful echoes in my head like thundering doom: *You should be careful, Celine.*

The mystery texts. Whoever's texting me, they're responsible for Rosalie and Teryn. I just know it.

And I'm on their list.

"Celine, what's wrong?" Brad says. "You just went white as a sheet. I was only kidding, you know."

"Yes. I'm okay," I force myself to reply. "I'm just shocked about Teryn, that's all. We were friends in college." There's no reason to make him worry about this. He's got enough problems of his own right now.

He nods sadly. "We're all too young to die."

I definitely agree with that.

I'm not going to tell him about the threatening texts, but there is something I want to ask him that may be related. "Not to change the subject, but I have a weird, totally out-of-the-blue question for you, if you don't mind," I say.

He smirks and folds his hands in his lap. "Go for it."

"Okay." There isn't really a way to work up to it, so I just come right out and ask. "When you lived in Nashau, did you know someone named Hannah Byers?"

I expect some kind of recognition, but I don't expect the curtain of cold fury that drops over his face. His eyes flash fire, his hands clench together until his knuckles turn white, and he blows a long, thin breath through slightly parted lips, like a woman trying to control labor pains.

"Why?" he finally grounds out. "What's she done now?"

I'm so taken aback that I almost can't catch my breath. "I don't know," I squeak. "She just bought a house from me, and—"

"Here? In Wolfsbrook?"

He practically shouts the questions, and I flinch. My mouth won't move enough to say yes, so I swallow hard and give a little nod.

Brad deflates as suddenly as the anger came over him, and he bows his head. "Jesus, I'm sorry," he rasps. "I swear I'm not mad at you. It's just that Hannah—" He breaks off and looks up with effort, and there are tears standing in his eyes. "She was my girlfriend in high school," he says in a low, horrified tone. "And she's the reason we moved here for my senior year. My parents wanted to get me away from her, because she was fucking psychotic."

"Psychotic how?" I whisper.

"I don't know, just crazy. She fucked with my head so much. And she did things . . ." He shakes his head. "For one thing, she was insanely jealous. She broke some girl's nose with her binder and then held her down and cut all her hair off, because she thought the girl was flirting with me when she'd asked to borrow a quarter for lunch. And that was in ninth grade." His throat works, and a tear snakes down his cheek. "She only got worse from there."

Oh my God, it's her. Hannah. She's the one who's been texting me.

She killed Rosalie.

"Brad, I'm so sorry." I slide forward in the chair and reach for his hands, taking them in mine. They're hot and trembling. My heart explodes with sympathy for him — I can't imagine what he's gone through with Hannah, but it was clearly hellish. "I didn't mean to upset you."

He squeezes his eyes shut, but another tear still falls. "Jesus, I can't believe she's in Wolfsbrook," he says. "I might have to get a restraining order or something. At least she hasn't been here yet. Celine . . . you have to stay away from her." His green eyes meet mine with desperation. "She's absolutely nuts. She gets in your head. Promise me you'll stay away."

"I promise." I don't tell him that she's already managed to get a job where I work, or that she claims to have a daughter she can't possibly have, with eerie similarities to mine. I've decided that I need to go to the police. Even if it means telling them about what happened with Joan. "And I'm sorry, but I have to go. There's something I need to take care of," I say. "I'll come back tomorrow, okay?"

He flashes me a wary look. "What is it? If it has something to do with Hannah . . ."

"Not really," I tell him, only half lying. It concerns Hannah, but I'm not going to deal with her directly. I'm just going to report her to the police. "It's just work stuff. And I promise I'll be back first thing tomorrow."

"I hope so." He smiles, but there's sadness in it. "Have I told you how much I missed you?"

Not as much as I've missed you. I almost say it, but at the last moment I realize that's in extremely poor taste. Brad might be trying to laugh about it, but I think it's too early for coma jokes. So I simplify things, and say, "I missed you, too."

His smile grows a fraction as he turns my hands over slowly. "No wedding ring."

"No. I'm not married," I say. "Or divorced, or engaged, or otherwise involved."

"You're single? I don't believe that."

"Well, it's true." I shrug it off. I'm aching to tell him that I'm single because the man I love has been in a coma for five years, but that's too much, too soon. And I have to see how he feels about Alyssa first, before I throw my heart back at his feet.

I'll tell him tomorrow. After I do something about Hannah.

Brad is still smiling, but exhaustion lurks in his expression. "I hope you won't be insulted if I don't get up to say goodbye," he says. "I think I've had enough standing this morning."

"Of course not. I completely understand." I get up instead and lean down to hug him.

He brushes his lips on my cheek. "You'll come back tomorrow?"

"Yes, I will."

It's harder than I expect to leave him, especially knowing what I have to do now. But at least I have something concrete to show the police. I'm hoping that, if nothing else, exposing Hannah will keep her away from Brad — and from me. And at best, if she really did kill Rosalie, she'll be arrested.

I think about poor Teryn as I walk past the nurses' station and wonder again what happened. How she died. It must not have been violent, since no one knew she was dead. And if she'd been murdered, I would've heard something about it by now, even in passing. So maybe this really was just a coincidence.

The elevator car I step into is empty, and I press the button for the parking garage level. I'm already trying to talk myself out of going to the police. But I have to, even though they'll probably make me talk to the detectives who came to my house.

Chambers and Garfield are on my mind, and not in a good way. So when the elevator doors open and the two of them are standing there outside the car, I'm so startled that I scream and stumble back.

It turns out that's the worst possible reaction I can have, because they came looking for me.

CHAPTER 18

The fact that I'm not in handcuffs isn't much of a consolation, and it doesn't keep me from crying out of pure fear as I sit alone in a locked room at the police station. I'm sure that bawling my eyes out isn't helping my case either, but that's the reason I can't help it. There shouldn't be a case at all.

Now they think I had something to do with Teryn.

At the hospital, the detectives told me that I wasn't being charged with anything, but that I had to come to the station with them and answer some questions. If I didn't go voluntarily, they said they'd get a warrant and arrest me. And they wouldn't let me take my own car. They'd put me in the back of a police car, refused to answer my questions or listen to me about Hannah, and then taken me to this room with a table, two chairs, a clock on the wall and a camera in a corner of the ceiling. A female officer came in and confirmed my name, my address and that I'd known Teryn Holmes, and then she took my purse and cell phone and left me here alone, locked in.

I've been here for hours. The clock says it is almost 1 p.m., and I am supposed to pick up Alyssa from school at quarter to three. What will happen if I'm not there? Will they have her stay there with the teacher? Put her on a bus and send her home to an empty, locked house? Call Social Services and take her away from her negligent mother?

By the time the door to the room opens a little after 1:30 and the female officer who talked to me before walks in, I'm frantic with worry. I try to swipe my face clean and look at her. "Excuse me. I'm sorry, but I really need to pick my daughter up from school soon," I tell her, my voice foggy and pathetic. "Will I be able to do that? She gets out at 2:45."

The officer glances at the clock and frowns. "Can she ride the bus home?"

"No. She's only four, she's in kindergarten," I say. "There's just me and her. She can't be home alone."

"It's still going to be a few minutes before the detectives can talk to you, and I don't know how long they'll take," the woman says. Her tone is businesslike, her stance rigid, but I hope I'm not imagining the slight warmth in her eyes. "Is there someone else you can call to pick her up?"

I struggle to keep my shattered hopes from showing. I don't want to call someone, I want to get out of here, pick up my daughter, and put this nightmare behind me. But at least I don't have to leave Alyssa stranded. "Yes, I can call someone," I say in a small voice. "Can I use my phone?"

"Here, you can use mine." The officer takes a cell phone from her belt, swipes at the screen a few times, and hands it to me. The dial pad is pulled up.

"Thank you," I manage as I tap in Jill's cell phone number. I only have two people on the list of adults allowed to get Alyssa from school in emergencies, and the other one is my mother. I don't want her to find out where I am, and why. I'll never hear the end of it.

Jill answers after three rings. "What's wrong, did you lose my desk number?" she says teasingly.

"Jill. I need a huge favor." A lump forms in my throat, and I turn my back and walk away from the officer, making my voice as quiet as possible. I'm sure she hears me anyway, but I don't want her to. "I'm sorry, I know you're at work . . .

but can you pick Alyssa up from school and watch her for a while? She gets out at 2:45."

"What happened?" Jill says, immediately concerned. "Are you okay, Celine?"

"No," I whisper. Fresh tears form in my eyes, and I squeeze them shut, trying to make it stop. "I mean, I'm not hurt or anything. Oh, God, it's a long story." I draw in a shuddering breath. "I'm at the police station, and I . . . can't leave yet."

"Oh, my God. Did those stupid bastards arrest you about Rosalie?" Jill nearly shouts. "This is ridiculous. Sweetie, you need to lawyer up, right now. I mean it. Don't say a word to them. I'll get Jeff to go down there, and—"

"Jill, wait. Just a second." Once again I'm grateful for her passion, but Jeff Lindstrom is a real estate lawyer. And if I do need a lawyer eventually, it'll have to be a criminal defense lawyer. The thought of that makes me shudder. "I'm not under arrest," I explain. "They want to ask me some questions. It's just taking longer than it should, for some reason."

"That means they're trying to find a reason to arrest you," Jill says. "Trust me, I know all about this. It's disgusting what they're doing. Do *not* answer any questions."

I know she's right, and I'm sickened that I don't seem to have much of a choice. "I really don't think Jeff can help," I say under my breath, walking further away from the officer. "I mean, he's in real estate."

"Yeah, but he still went to law school. He knows enough to get you out of there."

The idea of refusing to answer questions when the police ask them, of exercising my right to a lawyer, is so terrifying that it leaves me dizzy. But they *are* looking for a reason to arrest me, and I can't let that happen. "All right. If he can get down here," I finally say. "But please, just get Alyssa for me. She's all I'm worried about."

"I will. That's one thing you *don't* have to worry about," Jill says. "We'll be waiting at your place for you, and I'll make sure you get there soon."

"Thank you," I say, my voice catching on the words.

She promises again that everything's going to be fine, and we hang up. As I turn to hand the phone back to the officer, I'm startled to see the detectives standing near the open door to the room. How long have they been here?

"Are you all set with your daughter?" the woman says.

I nod. "Yes, my friend's picking her up. Thank you."

She doesn't say that I'm welcome. She just returns her phone to her belt, walks past the detectives, and leaves the room, closing the door behind her.

I swallow and move toward the table on unsteady legs, and all but collapse in one of the chairs. Even though it's proven pointless to talk to them so far, I give it another shot anyway. "I tried to tell you before that I was just coming down here to talk to you," I say. "I think I might know who killed Rosalie."

"Really. Do you think this same person killed Teryn Holmes?" Chambers pulls the other chair away from the table, turns it around, and sits backwards to stare at me. "Because we think *you* did. She was poisoned, and someone attempted to make it look like a suicide. Again."

"Oh my God," I whisper, not even trying to stop the tears. "She *is* crazy. She killed them both."

The detectives look at each other. Garfield opens his mouth, but I cut him off with a surge of desperate bravado. "My phone," I blurt. "I've been getting threatening texts. Just look at it. Hannah Byers killed them, and she's threatening me too, because of Brad."

"All right," Garfield says slowly. "We'll check it out."

He leaves the room, and I shudder beneath Chambers' drilling glare. "Please. I didn't kill anyone," I say, wincing as I remember that I'm not supposed to talk to them until Jeff gets here. But I'm not answering any questions — I'm telling them what I planned to in the first place. "I'm sorry I screamed like that at the hospital. It's just that I was already coming to talk to you, and . . . well, there you were. It scared me."

Chambers' features seem to ease a little, but I can't tell for sure. "If you were receiving threatening texts, why didn't you report it?" he says. "Especially if you knew who was sending them."

"I didn't know who it was. Not until this morning, when I talked to Brad," I tell him. My heart is hammering like a drum, but I can't freeze up this time. "Hannah . . . she's his ex-girlfriend, from high school. He says she was crazy jealous. And she was just discharged from a psychiatric hospital a few weeks ago, before she came to Wolfsbrook. She was there for five years. Again, I didn't know any of this when I was getting the texts. They're from an anonymous number."

The detective's eyebrows go up. "You're sure about all this?"

"Positive," I say.

Garfield comes back in with my phone and hands it to me. I unlock the screen, tap through to the message thread, and wince as I read the first one again. *I know what you did. Murderer.* "I'm not a murderer," I say as I give the phone slowly to Chambers. "Like I said, she's crazy. But . . . she's not talking about Rosalie or Teryn."

Chambers looks at the screen while Garfield reads over his shoulder. After a long minute, Chambers glances at me. "Who is she talking about, then?"

I sigh and bite my lip. "Joan Carpenter. We went to the same college, and she . . . well, she started this little group. The Brad Dowling Fan Club. And I found out about it."

The whole story comes out. How I'd stumbled across a tiny, private online forum in my freshman year of college — I'd bought used textbooks, and someone had scribbled the URL in the margin of my biology book — found out it was all about worshipping Brad, who I was already friends with at the time, and decided to join for a laugh. How gushy and silly and sad it had all seemed. There were only about a dozen users, and all of them were anonymous, with handles like IHeartBrad and Brad4Life. But I'd 'befriended' the forum owner and president, and she told me her real name.

That was when I showed Brad the forum and told him who'd started it. And it turned out he had an elective with Joan — they were both sophomores at the time — and he'd confronted her about his 'fan club' in front of the whole class. I wasn't there, of course, but people said she'd been completely humiliated and fled the classroom in tears.

The next morning, Joan was found dead in her dorm room. She'd hung herself, after she wrote a long, miserable post on the forum about how ruined her life was now that everyone knew the pathetic truth, and she would never have a chance with Brad.

"I didn't kill her," I say as the detectives look on, stone-faced. "But it's my fault she's dead. What I did was stupid and mean, and I was probably trying to impress Brad, even then. I'll feel responsible for Joan's death all my life . . . but I'm not a murderer."

Neither of them says anything for a moment, and I start to think maybe there's a way they can arrest me for Joan's death. But then Chambers leans forward and sighs. "So you think this Hannah knows what happened, and now she's targeting you," he says. "What was her last name, again?"

"Byers. Hannah Byers," I tell him. "And yes, that's what I think. I found a newspaper photo online of her and Joan together at an Oslow State game. They knew each other."

"What about the rest of these forum users, the fan club?" Garfield says. "Is the forum still active? We may have to look into all of them, and anyone who's been involved with Brad Dowling. I hate to say it, but this does seem to be an ex-girl-friend out for revenge."

I actually laugh, surprising myself. "Well, Detective, good luck with that," I say. "I'm sorry. I guess you don't know that Brad dated about half the juniors and seniors in high school during the year he was there, and probably twice that many girls once he got to college. Most of them still live around here."

Chambers groans aloud. "Nothing's ever easy, is it?" he says, shaking his head. "All right, Ms. Bauman. It would be very helpful if you could point us to that forum and anything else you find online. And we'll need to have the tech department go through your phone, to see if they can trace the source of these texts. Is that going to be a problem?"

"No, it's fine." I can grab a pay-as-you-go phone and have my number temporarily transferred. And I'm happy to let them find out who's doing this. "Does this mean I'm not a suspect anymore?"

"You weren't a suspect. You were a person of interest," Garfield says.

I don't believe him, but I'll let it go for now. "What about Hannah?"

"I think we'd better question her right away," Chambers says with a glance at his partner, who nods in agreement. "As in now. Do you have an address for her?"

I nod and tell them the address of the Quintaine property. "I'm sure it's her. It has to be," I say. "Everything lines up."

"Are you a detective now, Ms. Bauman?" Chambers' brows quirk into a sardonic lift.

My face heats up, and I hope it's not as red as it feels. "No, of course not. I just . . ."

"Don't worry. If she doesn't have a rock-solid alibi, we'll bring her right in," he says. "We'll make sure you're protected."

Somehow I don't feel safer knowing that. After all, they haven't done a great job at figuring out what happened to Rosalie and Teryn so far — they thought *I* killed them. And I've found out more about what's really going on than they have. But I won't mention that, because maybe they'll arrest me for insulting them or something.

Apparently they can do that. I'm finding out all sorts of things I never knew the police could do, along with a few things they can't do.

Like find the right people who've committed a crime.

Garfield takes my phone from Chambers. "I'll get this into processing," he says. "Meet you outside?"

Chambers nods and stands as his partner walks from the room. "Sit tight, Ms. Bauman."

"Wait. You're not leaving me here again, are you?"

"Only for a minute. I'll have Officer Koch come in to take your statement, and then you're free to go," he says. "She can take you back to your car, if you'd like."

"All right." I assume Officer Koch is the woman who let me use her phone. "Will you let me know what happens with Hannah? I'm going to have my number switched to another phone, so you can still contact me."

"We'll keep you as informed as possible," he says, which doesn't answer my question.

He leaves the room, and I lace my fingers together and squeeze hard. I will not cry. Not anymore. And even though I'm being let go, and the detectives are going to talk to Hannah right now, I have no faith in their ability to stop any of this.

So I'll have to do it myself.

CHAPTER 19

It's almost seven by the time I make it home with my car, a replacement phone and a gut full of raw, thrumming nerves. Jill's already gotten Alyssa fed, bathed and in her pajamas, and I let her stay up half an hour past her bedtime so I can see her longer. I don't tell her what's happening — I just say that I had a work emergency and apologize half a dozen times for not being here. I feel terrible lying to my daughter.

But she's far too young to understand any of this, and she'll only be frightened.

Jill stays the whole time while I tuck Alyssa in, read her an extra story and spend a long time hugging her. When I come out from the bedrooms, she has a bottle of chilled wine and two glasses set out on the coffee table. "I think you can use some of this," she says.

"Absolutely. You're a lifesaver," I breathe as I collapse on the couch and scrub a hand down my face. "God, what a nightmare. Thank you *so* much for helping me with all this."

Jill frowns slightly as she pours the wine and hands me a glass. "I'm sorry about Jeff," she says. "I can't believe he wouldn't go down there. I was trying to find another lawyer for you, and . . . you know, I almost sent Danny." She snorts and rolls her eyes. "If I'd done that, you'd probably still be there."

"It's fine. I got out of it," I say, sipping the cold, sweet wine with relief. "Thank you for trying, though."

"No problem." Jill lifts her own glass and drinks. "And you really didn't answer any questions?"

I shake my head. "I didn't give them a chance to ask. I had plenty to tell them."

"Yeah, about that." She scooches closer, her eyes wide. "Now you have to tell *me*. Something about that Hannah chick being batshit nuts?"

Laughing feels good after all I've been through today, even though nothing about Hannah is funny. I've only told Jill a tiny bit about the whole mess, because I didn't want Alyssa to hear it.

So I give her the story.

By the time I finish, we've both drained two glasses of wine and Jill is pouring herself a third. "Holy God, she is one screwed-up princess," she says after a moment. "Do you think she killed her parents, so she could get their money?"

I give a startled blink. I hadn't even considered that, but if she really killed two women just because they used to date Brad, maybe she was capable of parent-cide too. "I don't know," I say. "They did say it was arson, and they never found the culprit."

"I'll bet she did. And then she hid out in the wacko hospital until things died down, so she could carry out the rest of her dastardly plans." Jill chuckles and gulps more wine. "Oh, boy. Or maybe I'm just drunk."

I shrug. "Who knows? There's so much crazy in all this, I wouldn't be surprised."

"Yeah, Wolfsbrook has our very own homicidal maniac." She sits back, raising an eyebrow. "So how did you get the cops to let you go? You never said."

A hot surge of guilt murders the nice buzz I'd been building. I haven't told Jill about the texts — or about Joan. But now that I've confessed to the police, maybe it's time I

115

came clean with my best friend. She deserves to know, even if she thinks I'm awful for doing it.

"The thing is . . . someone's been threatening me," I say in a faltering tone.

"What?" Jill looks horrified. "How? Since when?" she says.

"I've been getting anonymous texts. It started the day of Rosalie's funeral," I admit softly. "The last one was Tuesday, when I went to see Brad. When Teryn died."

"Oh, my God. Why didn't you tell me?"

"I couldn't." I take a slow breath, shaking as I let it out. "Whoever it is, probably Hannah, they know something I did. Something I'm ashamed of."

Despite my resolution to stop crying about all this, tears prick my eyes. I blink them back. Damn it, I'm going to be strong. I *have* to be.

"Honey," Jill says gently, giving my free hand a squeeze. "Whatever it is, I doubt you need to be ashamed of it. You can tell me."

Yes, I do need to be ashamed. I can't let myself off the hook for this. I did this thing, and I have to own up to it, because it was wrong. But what I *don't* have to do is keep beating myself up over it. I can feel bad without letting it control my life.

And I can tell Jill without going to pieces. So I do.

I keep my explanation short. She listens, her lips twitching a few times. And when I get to the end of the story, she bursts out laughing.

"Oh, no, I'm sorry!" she stammers, still giggling. "I'm sorry. It's not funny that she's dead. Not even a little. It's just . . . a fan club, for *Brad*?" Another full-throated laugh bursts from her, and she claps a hand over her mouth. "It's mostly the wine, I swear. And I'm a horrible person for laughing. Okay, I'm going to stop now. Promise."

I try not to, but I can't help smiling. "It was kind of funny."

"Kind of?" Jill spurts with a giggle. Then she sobers and looks at me. "Celine, you can't blame yourself for that. You really can't."

"I have to," I say. "If I hadn't told Brad—"

"Then she would've found some other way to humiliate herself," Jill says firmly. "Come on. She was in college, and still writing gushy 'do you like me' notes with glittery stickers and doodle hearts. She was just doing it online instead of in a notebook. One way or another, people would've found out." She shakes her head. "You couldn't have known that she'd kill herself over it. No one could know that, except her."

Maybe she's right, but I'll never know for sure. At least I feel better for confessing.

Jill sighs and picks up the mostly empty wine bottle. "Crap. Do you mind if I crash on your couch tonight?" she says. "I don't think I should drive. Neither should you, after the day you've had."

"Of course I don't mind." I throw an arm around her, and she hugs me back. "You're the best," I say. "Let me grab some stuff for you."

I get up and gather extra pillows and blankets, and a t-shirt and shorts for Jill to sleep in, and bring them out to the living room. We stay up talking a while longer, until the wine is completely gone and we're both too exhausted to keep our eyes open, and then I head for my bedroom while she settles on the couch. Once I'm changed and under the covers, I fall asleep almost instantly.

What seems like five minutes later, I'm startled awake by an unfamiliar sound. It's the replacement phone. I haven't bothered changing any of the settings, and the default ringtone is some obnoxious, cheerful techno-pop style tune.

I scowl and blink at the alarm clock as I fumble the phone off the nightstand. It's just after eleven, and I have no idea who'd be calling me this late. The display on the screen is just a phone number that gives me no clue, but at least I know it's not the mystery text number.

I tap answer and bring the phone to my ear. "Hello?" I murmur.

"Ms. Bauman? It's Detective Chambers. Sorry to wake you."

Suddenly I *am* awake. My heart pounds in my throat, and I sit up too fast, making myself dizzy. "Is something wrong?" I say.

"Not exactly." The detective sounds terse and tired. "I just wanted to let you know that we've questioned Hannah Byers and investigated her alibis, and she checks out. We have no cause to hold her."

But she did it! I manage not to say that out loud. "Okay, so . . . now what?" I say as my mouth goes dry.

"We're not without suspicion, and we're continuing the investigation into her," he says. "But now we'll also have to interview Mr. Dowling, get a list of his exes, and start talking to all of them. This is going to take time."

"Meanwhile, there's still someone threatening me," I say.

"Yes, I'm aware of that. We're hoping to get something from your phone," he says. "All I can tell you is that if you don't feel comfortable around Ms. Byers, you should avoid her for the time being. And call us if you see anything suspicious or find any proof."

Avoiding Hannah isn't exactly going to be easy, since she's just gotten herself a job at my office. But it doesn't matter. The police aren't going to help me. I'm on my own.

"All right. Thank you, Detective," I say. "I appreciate the information."

"We'll let you know when we get the results from your phone," he says. "Goodnight, Ms. Bauman."

"Goodnight."

I hang up and toss the phone on the nightstand, falling onto the bed with a sigh. I'm not getting back to sleep anytime soon.

CHAPTER 20

This morning I realize that I'm grateful Alyssa has started school. I feel bad about that, but knowing that she's safe while I deal with the nightmare that's invaded my life is a tremendous relief. I can't imagine having to drag her around through all of this. She would be so scared.

Before we leave the house, I take a few pictures of her with the new phone. I'm going to need them soon. Hannah isn't the only thing I have to handle today.

Once I drop my daughter off for the day, I head straight for the real estate office, hoping Hannah isn't there yet. When I arrive, only Maxine's car is in the lot. Good. I need to tell her what's happening and insist that she fire Hannah. I can't be around her.

As I'm walking inside, I change my mind about telling Maxine — but for once, it's not because of my fear of confrontation. I decide that I *want* to confront Hannah. Put it all out there and see how she reacts. I need to know the truth, because if the police aren't going to do anything, I have to protect myself.

Maybe she does have solid alibis. Maybe she's really innocent, and there's someone else entirely I have to worry about. But there's definitely something wrong with Hannah.

Maxine's office door is closed. I knock, and then open the door without waiting for her to respond. She's at her desk, on her computer, and she leans aside and blinks at me. "Come on in, Celine."

"That's what I was doing." I ignore the sarcasm in her voice as I walk to her desk. My hands are clammy and trembling, but I'm not going to give in to the fear. I need to grow a spine, right now. "Will Hannah be here today?"

"Yes, she's coming in this afternoon," Maxine says, looking at me curiously. "I want her to go with you while you stage the new listing, so she can see how it's done. Is that going to be a problem?"

"It's fine." I'm surprised that my voice doesn't shake, that I sound calm and confident. "Listen, I have something to do this morning," I say. "I'll be back later to get Hannah. If you see her before I do, could you remind her that she'll need to wear something she doesn't mind getting dirty? I want her to be hands-on, all the way."

Maxine arches one perfectly sculpted eyebrow. "I'll do that," she says. "Are you all right, Celine?"

"I'm fantastic." I flash her a brittle smile to prove it. "Oh, and tell Sabrina that if I don't have my half of the commission for the Quintaine sale by the end of the day, I'm going to sue her. The closing wrapped up days ago. See you in a few hours, Maxine."

I turn and walk from the office, leaving my boss with her mouth hanging open. I'm flushed and my pulse is racing, but I feel good. I am officially Getting Things Done.

Now I have another massive item I need to tackle, and this one's going to hurt.

I drive to the hospital. By now I know the way to Brad's room easily enough, and I navigate halls and elevators and corridors like a pro. He's expecting me this morning, since I told him I'd come back, and he's in the wheelchair watching a news show on the overhead television when I come into the room. He grabs a remote from the bed and turns the TV off, facing me with a smile. "Hey, pretty woman," he says.

My heart constricts as the old term of endearment leaves his lips. But I don't cry. I walk to him and hug him in the chair, so he doesn't have to get up, and then take a seat while he maneuvers around to face me. When he's close enough, I take his hand. "There's something I have to tell you."

"Oh, no." His face falls. "It's about Hannah, isn't it?"

"No. She's not going to be a problem," I say, hoping I sound confident enough. I'm determined to make sure she isn't a problem. "This is about my daughter."

I can't believe I came right out and said that. But there's no easy way.

The rest of the color drains from Brad's already washed-out face. "Your . . . daughter?"

"Yes. Her name is Alyssa." I'm still holding his hand as I ease the phone from my pocket and open the pictures, flipping to the best one. The one that shows her smiling face — and her beautiful green eyes. "She's four, almost five," I say, watching Brad for a reaction as I hand the phone to him. "This is her."

He reaches out, takes the phone and straightens it as he draws it closer. Then he lets out a sharp gasp and starts shaking. His eyes glaze over with tears as he pulls away from me to grip the phone with both hands. "Her eyes," he whispers. "Oh, God. She's . . ."

I swallow as my own tears start to flow, but I make no move to wipe them away. I'm not ashamed of this. "I didn't know that night," I say softly. "Not until about a week after the accident. Then my period was late, and I started feeling sick, and . . ." A smile drifts across my face. "She was born October 12. Not quite nine months later — she was a few weeks premature."

The phone falls from his hands to drop in his lap, and he raises his stricken features to meet my eyes. "I'm a father?" he rasps.

"Yes. I'm sorry," I say. "Not that I have her, but that I couldn't tell you. And when you woke up, you were already dealing with so much . . ." My voice trails off, and I clear my throat. "I'm not asking for child support or anything like that. I don't want you to think of this as manipulation, or emotional blackmail, or whatever. It's just . . . you deserve to know."

His chest hitches, and the tears finally spill from his eyes. "Celine," he says thickly as the corners of his mouth relax in what's almost a smile. "She's so beautiful. Just like her mother," he whispers. "I hope . . . you'll let her meet me. I'd like to get to know her, if that's okay with you."

I forget how to breathe.

I expected him to be miserable, horrified, maybe even angry. At best, I thought he might ask me to leave so he could think about the enormous bomb I'd dropped on him. But he wants to meet her. He wants to see my daughter. *Our* daughter.

I stand up, intending to hug him. But my legs give out and I drop to the floor, landing on my knees in front of him with a wrenching sob. He reaches for me, alarmed, and I shake my head and look up at him.

"She's amazing," I say. "Healthy, happy, *so* smart. You're going to love her."

He smiles, though he's still crying. "If she's part of you, then I already do."

It's too much, and I lose it completely.

I lay my head in his lap, shaking with the force of my emotions. He holds me awkwardly, comforts me, and for a long time after I'm done, I don't want to move. It's not fair that he had to miss so much of her life. But it means more than the world to me that he's willing to try now.

Eventually I get off the floor and take my seat back. I can't stay much longer, but I spend a few minutes telling him more about Alyssa and assuring him that we're doing fine, and we can take all of this slowly. By the time I have to leave, both of us are almost easy with each other.

There's one more thing I have to let him know. "The police are going to come and talk to you," I say, after briefly mentioning Hannah. "Probably today. They need a list of all your ex-girlfriends."

He grimaces. "Ugh. That's a long list," he says. "Why?"

"Because of Rosalie and Teryn." If he doesn't already know, the detectives will tell him anyway, so he may as well hear it from me. "They think their deaths weren't accidental, and that maybe the same person was involved."

Brad recoils like he's been punched. "You mean they were murdered?"

"That's the theory," I say. "They're looking at—"

"Hannah. It *must* have been her," he nearly growls. "That psychotic bitch. I can't believe she'd . . ." He trails off with a shiver. "I knew she was crazy," he mutters. "But honestly, I never thought she'd actually kill anyone. Do you think it was her?"

I'm not going to say what I think. If I tell him I'm planning to confront her, he won't like it. "The police investigated her, and they said they're suspicious but she has solid alibis," I tell him. "That's why they want to talk to everyone else."

"Well, I wouldn't count her out yet." His gaze unfocuses as he stares into the distance. "Jesus, Hannah. How many times . . ." He shakes himself and looks at me, halfway to smiling. "So, what do I tell them about you?" he says. "Are you my ex?"

"I don't know," I reply, matching his teasing tone. "I mean, we never officially broke up. So . . . am I?"

He clutches the arms of the wheelchair and pushes to his feet. It seems a lot easier for him to stand now. "I'd rather you weren't, actually," he murmurs as he takes a step toward me. "My ex, I mean. I'd really like you to be my now."

His hands settle on my waist, and I slip my arms around him. "Are you asking me out, Mr. Dowling?" I say.

"No. I'm asking you to stay." One hand comes up to caress my face, and I shiver pleasantly. "Stay mine, Celine," he whispers. "I never should've walked away from you."

I lean into him. "I can do that."

He groans and kisses me, a proper kiss. "Come back tomorrow?"

"Tomorrow, or the next day," I tell him with regret. I can't be sure how long it will take to deal with Hannah, but I want to be sure she doesn't cause any problems for me. For us. "We've got time now."

He agrees reluctantly, and after a few more very nice goodbyes, I head out. His mother will be swooping in soon, anyway, and I'd rather not get hit by her broomstick. But the next time I see her, I won't run. The new Celine doesn't run from problems.

No matter how hard they are to face.

I'm alone in the elevator, headed for the parking garage when my phone rings. This time I recognize Detective Chambers' number and answer right away.

"Ms. Bauman, we've got the results from your phone," he says. "The number those texts came from is impossible to trace. It's one of those free disposable ones you can sign up for online. We're putting pressure on the company that supplies the numbers to dig through their records, but it's slow going." He pauses, and adds, "But the lab did find something else."

"What?" I say, just as the elevator dings and the doors open.

"Where are you?" Chambers says.

"The hospital. I was visiting Brad."

"Did you tell him we're going to interview him?"

"Yes." I don't care if he doesn't like it.

But he just says, "Good. That'll make things easier, if he knows we're coming."

"Glad to help," I say as I step off the elevator and start across the glass walkway to the garage. "What about my phone?"

He sighs. "There's a hidden tracking app installed on it. We're not sure yet when it was placed, but . . . it tracks the phone's location, records calls and texts, and it allows for remote access to the phone, including Facebook. Which you have installed and logged in."

I'm so horrified, I have to stop walking for a minute. "Someone's been listening to my calls and tracking my phone?" I gasp.

124

"I'm afraid so. And this app is even harder to trace than the disposable number."

A hard shudder nearly drops me. At least that explains the text I got when I visited Brad the first time. They knew I was at the hospital.

"What should I do?" I say as I get moving toward my car again.

"For starters, keep using the phone you have," he says. "Have you noticed anything else behaving strangely, as far as electronics? Any problems with computers or laptops?"

My heart sinks as I remember the license fiasco, how the auto-fill was disabled and the computer skipped and lagged so much, with that weird, fast-blinking cursor. And I recall that it's done that more than once after the license thing. I never thought anything of it. "My computer at work," I say. "There's something wrong with it."

"Do you mind if we pick that up and bring it to the lab for testing?"

"No, take it. I want this person found."

Unless I find her first.

Detective Chambers assures me that everything will be fine, and I hang up still not believing him. But I'm going to change that.

I'm actually looking forward to confronting Hannah.

CHAPTER 21

The police make it to Hughes Real Estate before I do, and my computer tower is gone when I get there, though they've left the monitor and mouse behind. Maxine, Sabrina and Courtney are clustered at the reception desk, talking in a huddle that breaks up when I walk in, and both Sabrina and Maxine start toward me.

"Celine, what's going on?" Maxine says with a shrill edge to her voice. "There were police officers here, and they took your computer. They said you gave them permission."

"Yes, I did." I move around my desk to the chair side and start opening drawers, looking for the digital camera I use for staging photos. "Where's Hannah?"

Sabrina stares at me, open-mouthed. "Who cares about Hannah? What about the *police*?"

I slam a desk drawer shut, making them both jump, and glare at Sabrina. "Who cares about the police?"

"What's gotten into you, Celine?" Maxine says. "You need to tell me what's going on. That computer is company property, and I'd better get it back."

For another minute I ignore her, and finally locate my camera. I straighten and toss it into my briefcase, and then walk back around the desk toward the other women. "The police are investigating a couple of murders," I say, watching the shock form on their faces. "They took my computer, because someone is targeting me. Someone who wants to fuck with my life and take everything away from me. That wouldn't be you, would it, Sabrina?" I add with a sugary-sweet smile.

Her jaw drops. "What are you saying? I never—"

"Muscled in on my commission, because you were jealous?" I say. "Of course you didn't. I just hope the police believe you, since they're going to question you."

Sabrina's mouth flaps open and shut like a beached fish, and her face turns several interesting colors. "Oh my God, did you tell them I murdered someone?" she finally gasps. "Are you *crazy*? I don't even know who you're talking about!"

"Sure you do. Rosalie Phillips and Teryn Holmes," I say. "But don't worry, Sabrina, I didn't tell them. They're just questioning all of Brad's ex-girlfriends. And I know how proud you are of being with Brad."

"Really, Celine," Maxine interjects. "I know you're upset about the Quintaine deal, but you're accusing Sabrina of murder?"

"I'm not accusing anyone. The police are," I say, throwing her a challenging look. "And I've got work to do right now. So . . . where's Hannah?"

Maxine finally backs off. "She's not coming in today," she says weakly. "She called and said she had a long night."

Yes, I'll bet she did. I hope they grilled her like a steak.

"Fine. I'll do the staging myself," I say. "And I'm sure the police will bring your computer back soon. By the way, Sabrina . . . I wouldn't leave town, if I were you. It'll look suspicious."

I walk out of the office, leaving them to gape at my back.

By the time I reach my car, the adrenaline has worn off and I'm badly shaken. But I don't regret anything I said in there. I know people are used to me being a doormat, so this new Celine who doesn't back down is going to be hard to take at first.

It's harder on me than it is on them. I'm still moving forward, but my spine isn't growing as fast as I'd like. Every confrontation takes more out of me than the one before. I start to hope that confidence is like a muscle, that it'll get stronger the more I use it. But I have my doubts.

When I'm calm enough to drive, I head across town to the new listing. This one is a four-bed, two-and-a-half bath Tudor that's not as elaborate as the Quintaines' Victorian — it doesn't have a pool, for one — but it's still very nice, and the owners are much friendlier. It sits on two partially wooded acres with a private pond in the back, and the interior is luxury everything. There's even a home theater with actual rows of seats.

Staging this place isn't difficult. Most of it is impeccably clean, and the owners have already moved out, so I don't have to work around anxious sellers as I wipe and dust the few areas that need it and take photo after photo. This part of my job relaxes me; I enjoy framing and snapping the perfect picture to showcase a room or a feature, getting those just-right shots that capture the character of a home. For a while I'm able to forget about everything that's going wrong.

But eventually reality intrudes, and it's time to head to the school. I'll get there early, but I don't mind waiting. I hit a drive-thru for coffee on the way back through Wolfsbrook and pull into the school parking lot around 2:30, planning to wait in the car until classes are dismissed.

My plans change when I spot a slender platinum-blond figure standing behind the fence next to the school, in almost the exact same spot I first saw her.

Hannah.

I grab my purse and phone, get out of the car, and make my way toward the school, fueled by growing rage at what she's done to Brad — and to me. She sees me coming when I reach the sidewalk, and she actually smiles and starts to wave.

At least until I'm close enough for her to see my face.

"Celine?" Her brow furrows into a question that she doesn't ask.

"Hello, Hannah." I stop on the other side of the fence, feeling my heartbeat in my ears and my pulse fluttering in my throat. "Did you have a nice chat with the police last night?"

Her red lips part in shock. "How did you . . ."

"Oh, I know all about you," I say. "Your parents, the fire, where you've been for the past five years. And I know about Brad," I grind out.

She takes a step back, her vivid blue eyes blinking rapidly. "What are you saying?"

"I'm not saying anything. Except that you're Brad's psycho ex-girlfriend, and two women who used to date him are dead." I fold my arms and meet her stare. "Do you even *have* a daughter?" I say. "You know what? Never mind, don't answer that. What I really want to know is, did the police bother to ask whether you sent those texts to me?"

"What texts?" she whispers. "Celine, I don't know what you're talking about."

"Yes, you do. You're trying to get back at Brad, and destroy me."

She gasps. Her red lips quiver, and her eyes gleam with tears. She stands there for a long moment with her model-perfect face twitching and turning red. Finally, she screams, "I didn't do anything!" Then she whirls and runs away, across the grass, leaving a trail of sobs behind.

Funny. She forgot to pick up her daughter.

CHAPTER 22

Alyssa and I are cleaning up from dinner that night when my phone rings. It's Jill. I tell my daughter that she can go ahead and pick a movie to watch, and that I'll finish up and bring dessert out. I wait until she's in the living room before I answer the call.

"Hey, honey," Jill says. "How are you holding up?"

"I'm still here," I say with a laugh. "Thanks again for last night, by the way."

"Totally no problem. Did they arrest anybody yet?"

I heave a breath. "They're not even close," I say. "But they've ruled out Hannah. She has alibis."

"Oh my God, seriously? She's so guilty it hurts."

I've been thinking about that, and I'm not entirely convinced anymore. Hannah seemed genuinely shocked when I confronted her. But then, Brad did say that she's manipulative, so maybe she's just that good.

Unfortunately, I do have to consider that it might not be her.

"I guess they're still suspicious, but they can't arrest her," I say to Jill as I take the last of the dishes from the dining room into the kitchen. "They're going around questioning all of Brad's exes now."

Jill laughs. "That's going to take a while."

"Tell me about it." I decide not to mention the conversation I had with Brad this morning . . . not yet. It's still too fresh, too *mine* to share. "Anyway, at least I've stopped getting texts," I say. "All this activity must be scaring Hannah, or whoever it is."

"You really don't think it's her now?" Jill says.

"Honestly, I don't know. But I can't worry about her."

"Well, okay. Just be careful," she says. "Celine, do you want me to come over and stay the night again? In case something happens."

My first instinct is to say yes. I'm still scared, even though I'm outwardly handling it better. But I can't turn Jill into a crutch. That's not fair to her, or me. "No," I say. "Thank you, but we'll be fine."

"Okay. If you're sure," she says. "In that case, I've got good news for you."

I smile. Good news is definitely welcome right now. "Lay it on me."

"You're not going to believe this." She pauses for effect. "I have a date tonight."

"No way!" I practically squeal. Jill hasn't been out on a date in almost a year. She tries to claim it's because work keeps her busy, but I know she just hasn't found anyone she's all that interested in. "With who?"

"Remember Hunter from Old City?"

"Oh my God. That smoking hot guy with the tattoos we met that night with Hannah?"

"Yep, him." I can hear the grin in her voice. "He's taking me to Bel Votre."

Holy crap. That's probably the most expensive restaurant in Oslow. If he's taking her to the city, he's probably serious. "Oh, wow. That's awesome, Jill," I say. "You'd better have an amazing time!"

"I think I will," she says. "But . . . are you sure you're okay, Celine?"

"I'm fine. And if you don't go, I might have to kick your ass," I say with a laugh.

She snorts. "Maybe I won't. Just because I'd really love to see you try."

"Go. Date Hunter. Have a good time," I say. "And tell me all about it tomorrow."

"Will do, dahling. Love you."

"Love you too."

I hang up and head for the freezer to scoop out bowls of strawberry ice cream. When I bring them to the living room, Alyssa is on the couch, watching *Nanny McPhee*. She turns and lights up as I walk toward her. "Ice cream!" she says. "Is it strawberry?"

"Is there any other kind?" I say, smiling as I sit next to her and hand her a bowl. "This is a great movie. I'm glad you picked it."

"Yes. It's funny," she says. "Izzy told me this is her favorite."

I'm glad that my daughter's made such a good friend already. I remember what she told me about Izzy the other night, how her mother doesn't like her, and wonder if I can do anything about it. "Hey, munchkin. Do you want to invite Izzy over to play sometime?"

"You mean here, at our house?" she says with a broad smile. "Yes! Can she come over tomorrow?"

"I don't know, sweetheart. That might not work," I say, sorry to disappoint her. "Tomorrow is Saturday, and you don't have school. We'd have to find out where Izzy lives and ask her mommy if it's okay to come over. How about you talk to her on Monday about it?"

"Okay," Alyssa says, happily enough. "But not her real mommy."

I frown slightly. "What about her?"

"We can't ask her real mommy." My daughter swings her legs and eats a spoonful of ice cream. "We have to ask her Mama Julie."

Julie. Where have I heard that name before?

"All right, then. We can talk to Izzy about all this on Monday."

Alyssa seems satisfied with that.

I'm still trying to remember where I've heard the name Julie when my phone rings, and the number on the screen is Detective Chambers. "I have to answer the phone, munchkin, okay?" I say, leaning over to kiss her forehead. "I'll be right back."

"'Kay," she mutters around a mouthful of ice cream.

She's really into the movie, and she hardly notices when I get up and walk into the dining room. "Detective," I say when I answer the phone. "How's it going?"

"Frustratingly slow," he sighs. "We've only checked on a third of the exes so far. But I wanted to tell you about your work computer."

"You found something on it, didn't you?"

"Yes. The same type of backdoor program that's on your phone," he says. "But it looks like this one was exclusively used for remote access."

I only have a vague idea of what that is, so I decide to ask him a specific question. "If I tried to renew my real estate license online from that computer, would whoever used that program be able to screw it up?"

The detective pauses. "Probably," he says. "They'd be able to get into your IP settings and reroute forms and data. There's a lot you can do with remote access."

"Okay." I let out a breath. "Well, thanks again."

"Listen, Ms. Bauman," the detective says uncomfortably. "I know we got off on the wrong foot, but . . . I'm sorry about all this. And I'm sorry I don't have better news for you, like that we've caught whoever's doing this. I promise, we're going to."

"It's fine. And I appreciate that," I say.

We hang up, and I head back to the living room to be with my daughter. My strawberry ice cream is melting, but I don't mind. It's still sweet.

Just like my revenge is going to be.

CHAPTER 23

I've decided to go to Hannah's housewarming party after all. The blunt approach didn't work out so well, so I'll switch tactics. I'll be her friend and tell her how understanding I am about Brad, and maybe she'll open up to me and confess. Or maybe I'll find out that it's not her, after all.

Either way, I intend to know the truth by the end of the night.

Jill isn't coming with me. I talked to her earlier in the day, and she had an incredible time with Hunter, but she sounded absolutely awful. She'd picked up a nasty cold from somewhere. When I said I was going to Hannah's, she insisted on coming along to help, but I told her to stay home and rest. It's not like I'll be alone with the crazy woman. She'll have a houseful of people, so it's the perfect time to approach her.

Now I'm pulling up to the curb, about half a block away from the Victorian mansion. It's about 7:30. I wanted to wait until after the party started, just to make sure someone else would be here. And there are plenty of people now. Cars fill the long driveway and spill out onto the street — it looks like she's invited half the neighborhood.

Alyssa is home with Tabitha, who's saved my life once again by being available at the last minute, and I've promised to pay her double for tonight.

When I get out of the car, I can hear laughter, splashing and chatter from behind the house. It sounds like most of them are in the massive in-ground pool that came with this place. The pool is heated, which was one of the major selling features, but tonight is unseasonably warm and they probably don't need the heat.

I head for the front door I've already opened so many times, but I'm not the one with the key anymore, so I ring the doorbell. A few minutes pass before I hear footsteps approaching, and then the door opens and a blond woman smiles out.

It's not Hannah. This woman is shorter, curvy instead of slender. Her hair isn't as blond, and her eyes are a pretty brown. She has dimples, and she seems very warm and friendly.

"You must be here for the party?" she says.

"Uh. Yes."

"Well, come on in." She stands back, and I walk into the foyer.

The house is furnished for the first time in years — and it's beautiful. A mix of modern and antique, with a lot of pale colors, rich woods and light, airy accents. The place looks ten times better than it ever did when the Quintaines lived here.

Either Hannah or her decorator has exceptional taste.

"Pretty much everyone is outside," the blond woman who greeted me says after she closes the door, and then holds out a hand. "I'm Julie, by the way."

Shock bubbles through me as I shake it. "Celine," I mutter.

Julie. That's the name my daughter said last night, the one I was trying to remember where I'd heard it. Mama Julie. Hannah had mentioned someone named Julie on the phone while I was talking to her about my license problem.

Julie lives with her. Is she family? An employee?

"It's nice to meet you, Celine," Julie says, still smiling. And then I finally notice the small hands wrapped around Julie's leg, and the little blond head hiding behind the woman. I'm not sure exactly where she fits into whatever arrangement Hannah and Julie have, but I know who she is.

I smile and crouch down a bit, trying to catch the shy little girl's eye. "You must be Izzy," I say. "I think you know my daughter Alyssa."

The little girl gasps in surprise. "You're Alyssa's mommy?" she says in a small, clear voice. She still doesn't look out from behind Julie.

"Oh, my. The famous Alyssa," Julie laughs. "We've heard a *lot* about her. Izzy loves her to pieces already."

A swell of pride moves through me as I straighten, thinking that the little girl will come out when she's ready. "I'm pretty sure the feeling is mutual. I've heard a lot about your daughter, too."

"She's *my* daughter," a familiar voice says behind me.

I nearly jump as I turn around and see Hannah watching me warily, as if she expects me to bite. Her nervous gaze moves from me to Julie, and then to the small, mostly hidden figure behind the other woman. "Alice, will you please come out and say hello to Celine?"

"Don't call me that. I'm Izzy!" The child speaks with surprising force. She leans aside without letting go of Julie's leg, until her face is in view — a small, delicate face, framed with winter-pale blond hair. Her eyes are the same shocking pool-blue shade as Hannah's, and they're narrowed in anger. "I told you, I don't like Alice," she says.

"I'm sorry," Hannah stammers. "Please, can you just come and meet Mommy's friend . . ."

"You're not my mommy. I hate you!" the little girl shouts, and then runs off into the house.

Hannah flinches and rests a hand on her heart with the other arm folded protectively across her stomach, her eyes wide and hurt.

"Oh, no. I'm so sorry, Miss Byers," Julie says in a small voice. "It's been stressful for her today. I'll speak to her about her manners."

"No. Don't reprimand her." Hannah sips in a shaking breath and stares after the little girl as the hand on her chest trembles. "I know it's going to take time. I just . . . after the other day, I thought we'd made progress."

Julie walks up to her and rubs her thin shoulder. "You did. She just had a setback," she says. "I'll go and get her."

Hannah shakes her head. "See if she's okay, but don't make her come out if she doesn't want to," she says. "We can try again tomorrow."

"All right." Julie gives her a gentle squeeze, nods to me, and then hustles off.

Now it's just me and Hannah in the foyer. She stares at me, biting her lip, and then lowers her arms to her sides in defeat. "My daughter. Alice Isabel," she says. "In case it's not obvious . . . she hates me."

She buries her face in her hands and bursts into tears.

I don't know what to do. I put an arm around her shoulders and steer her into the parlor off to the left, which is furnished but empty of people. She's crying harder than ever, and my pity outweighs any lingering doubts I have about her. And there's no one else to comfort her.

So I hug her. At first she stiffens, but then she starts to relax against me. Soon she's resting her head on my shoulder, clinging to me like an anchor as sob after heartbreaking sob wrenches from her chest.

She finally dwindles into wretched sniffles and pulls back, swiping at her ruined face. "Oh, God, I'm such a trainwreck," she says in a voice like a foghorn. "This party was a stupid idea. And this house, and this town, and . . ."

"Hey, take it easy." I try to smile as I dig around in my purse and find the pack of travel tissues I keep for emergencies. This qualifies. "Do you want to sit down?" I say, handing them to her.

She nods, fumbles a tissue loose and blows her nose, a big, honking blast. "Ugh. That's so disgusting," she says as she walks unsteadily toward a rich, cream-colored Chesterfield sofa with walnut trim. She practically collapses at one end and drops the used tissue into an oval vanity wastebasket tucked discreetly beside the back leg. "I'm sorry, Celine."

"No, *I'm* sorry." I take a few steps in her direction and gesture at the couch. "Mind if I sit with you?"

She shakes her head as she wiggles another tissue free. "Please. Have a seat."

I take the other end, leaving a bit of space between us so it's not too weird. "I shouldn't have said all that to you yesterday," I tell her. "I was just . . ."

"Yes, you should have. I deserved it." She wipes her cheeks, blows her nose again and tosses the tissue, immediately taking a fresh one out. "I'm awful," she says, staring at her lap. "I'm the worst kind of person — a fake everything with a lot of money. Fake mom, fake friend, fake real estate agent." She lifts her head slowly with a terrible, watery smile. "Fake app developer. I lied to you about that," she says.

For some reason, that surprises me more than anything else she's said so far. "You pretended that you made an app?"

"Yeah. Stupid, right?" She looks down again. "I read somewhere about how easy it was supposed to be. And I did watch some tutorials, and I tried. But I couldn't make anything work," she says, laughing bitterly. "So I downloaded this dumb, obscure app that hardly anyone knew about and started saying that I developed it. I guess . . . I wanted people to think I was smart, or cool, or something."

I can sympathize with that.

"Anyway, now you know the truth. I'm sad and worthless," she sighs. "Alice — I mean, Izzy — I can see why you thought I was lying about having a daughter. It must've been weird seeing me hang around the school by myself, right?"

"Yes, it was pretty weird," I say.

"Julie does everything for her. Takes her to school, makes her meals, tucks her in at night. I just go to watch sometimes, that's all." Hannah closes her eyes. "Everything you said about me was right. I was at Seton-Frischer before I came here, and I . . . don't have a daughter. Not really." She shudders.

I bite my lip. "Do you want to talk about it?"

"I think I should explain it, at least," she says, and looks at me. "She *is* my daughter. I was pregnant when I got committed, but I couldn't keep her. You know, mental hospital and all." She flashes a dark smile. "I didn't want to give her up, either. So I found Julie and hired her to work for me. To take care of my daughter until I was released. I figured that once I had my shit together, I'd take her back and we'd be a happy little family. But . . . Julie's the only mother she's ever known," she finishes in a whisper. "I keep trying, but it's so hard to get through to her."

"Well, I can see that you love her," I say. "You're doing a great job, being very patient in difficult circumstances. I think she'll come around eventually."

"Really?" A tentative smile lifts her lips. "Thank you, Celine. That means a lot to me," she says. "And I'm so glad that our daughters are friends."

"Maybe we can be, too," I say.

"I'd like that." She sniffles and looks away again. "By the way . . . about Brad."

My breath catches. "What about him?"

"I can't tell you how sorry I am for the way I treated him," she says in a paper-thin voice. "I was a terrible, spoiled child who never had to grow up, so I didn't. I acted out in high school, a *lot*. And poor Brad was right in the middle of my shitstorm." Her shoulders tense as she hunches away. "I lost my shit when his family moved away, and my parents sent me to a 'teen retreat' for my senior year," she says, making air quotes around the words. "That place actually helped me a lot. I was so much better . . . at least, until the fire. Then I lost it even harder."

I'm starting to feel really awful for her, and guilty for thinking of her as a crazy rich bitch. She obviously has reasons to act the way she does. "Every kid makes mistakes," I say. "Sometimes they make really bad ones."

"Yeah. But my mistakes were the worst." She unclenches and looks at me tentatively. "How is he doing? Brad, I mean."

"Surprisingly well."

"That's good," she says. "He hates me, doesn't he?"

I decide not to answer that.

She takes my silence as assent. "Of course he does. Why wouldn't he?" she rasps. "Ever since I heard he woke up, I've thought about going up there. To apologize for being so horrible. But I don't think he'll listen to a word I say . . . and I don't blame him."

I can't bring myself to contradict her, because she's probably right. Instead I say, "The most important thing is for you to forgive yourself."

"That's what my therapist says." She laughs weakly. "Oh, well. I guess I'd better get back to the party, if I can manage to make myself presentable," she says. "Thank you for talking to me, Celine. I don't . . . really have any friends."

"Well, now you do," I tell her.

She smiles. "Do you think you can stay? Just for a little while. If you can't, I understand."

"Sure," I say. "I'll stay."

I'm convinced that Hannah isn't behind the texts or the murders. But even though I'm relieved that the police haven't let the real culprit go, I've got a whole new layer of worries to replace that relief.

Because if it's not Hannah, then who *is* it?

140

CHAPTER 24

Alyssa is watching cartoons, and I'm in the kitchen making pancakes for a lazy Sunday brunch, when my phone rings. I almost don't bother looking at it since my hands are covered with flour. But I wipe them on my jeans and pick up the phone from the counter, and see Detective Chambers' number.

I figure I'd better answer.

"Ms. Bauman, I'm actually calling with good news," he says after I greet him. He sounds exhausted. "We've made an arrest for the murder of Teryn Holmes."

"You have?" My mind races as I try to guess which of Brad's ex-girlfriends has flipped her shit. But I can't come up with any likely suspects. "Who?"

"Kate Engle. She's a nurse at Hayhurst, a co-worker of Teryn's," he says. "Apparently they've had some kind of rivalry for years, and Teryn attempted to file a restraining order against Engle. We found Nembutal and chloroform hidden in Engle's work locker. The poisons that were in Teryn's system."

I didn't recognize the name at all. "So she's not Brad's ex?"

"No. This was completely personal," Chambers says. "Nothing to do with Mr. Dowling."

Something about this seems wrong. I have no idea who Kate Engle is, but it seems convenient for the detectives to find a murder weapon, or whatever they considered poison, in a locker five days after the murder was committed. But if I mention that to Chambers, he'll probably remind me that I'm not a detective.

Instead I ask, "What about Rosalie?"

"We're revisiting that case, but we're considering the possibility that it may have been a suicide after all," he says. "Handwriting matches are rarely conclusive. And to be honest, it was only a hunch."

"What was a hunch?"

Chambers clears his throat. "The suicide, thinking it was murder," he says. "It was my hunch, actually. After we interviewed the family and friends, the suicide note didn't make sense — the idea that she killed herself over a man she hadn't been involved with in years. That's why I had the handwriting analyzed." He sounds awkward and embarrassed as he explains. "Things seemed to fit when there wasn't a match. And then Teryn Holmes was apparently murdered, and there was a connection between the two victims. A thin one." He blows out a breath. "I was following my instincts. But it must've been a coincidence."

"Maybe you should trust your instincts."

"I did," he says, startling me a bit. I hadn't realized I'd said that out loud. "Unfortunately, the chief trusts evidence, not instincts. We found evidence. So the case is closed."

Suddenly I hear the bitter note behind his words, and I realize he doesn't buy the convenient poison-in-the-locker theory either. They've arrested the wrong person — again. But this time it's not Detective Chambers' fault. "What if the chief is wrong?" I say.

"The chief is never wrong. Just ask him," Chambers says with a rueful laugh. But then he grows serious. "As a police officer, I'm officially telling you that the case is closed. But as a guy who's interviewed a woman clearly terrified for her life, a guy who trusts his instincts . . . I'm telling you to be careful."

I close my eyes as a chill prickles my skin. "I will be," I say. "Thank you, Detective Chambers."

"Oliver. Ollie, if you like that better," he says. "I'm just a concerned guy now."

"All right. Ollie." Something close to despair wells inside me. If he's just a guy, and the killer is still out there, I have no one to protect me. "And I'm Celine," I say. "Just a woman terrified for her life."

My voice cracks on the last few words, and Ollie says, "I'm so sorry, Celine. If there was anything I could do . . ." He trails off, and I hear him curse in the background. "Look, you have my number. You can still call me if you need anything."

"Maybe I'll do that." I manage a smile. "I'd better go before my pancakes burn."

"Mmm, pancakes. The perfect breakfast," he says. "Celine, I hope you'll keep in touch."

"I will," I tell him.

We say goodbye, and I tuck the phone in my pocket as I turn back to breakfast-in-progress. At least I have my pancakes. But I don't have what I need the most — a clue about who's been killing my friends and threatening me with vague promises to ruin my life.

I freeze with the spatula in my hand. The texts. If a woman I've never met killed Teryn, and no one killed Rosalie . . . then who's been texting me?

It's too late to point that out to Ollie. Even if I had, he wouldn't be able to do anything about it. The police have closed the case. But there's still someone out there, with me in their sights, and I don't think this false arrest is going to stop them.

In fact, it'll probably encourage them.

I finish making the pancakes and bring two plates to the living room. Sundays are quiet days for me and Alyssa, and we almost always have a late, casual TV breakfast and then hang around the house or go to the park for a while, with no big plans.

But today I think we might do something different. I told Brad that if I didn't visit him yesterday, I would today.

And I could leave Alyssa with a sitter, but I always feel guilty doing that.

So maybe it's time for my daughter to meet her father.

* * *

Alyssa is her usual bubbly self as we walk down the fifth-floor corridor to room 548. She doesn't fear hospitals yet, because she's never had to be in one. All she knows is that we're going to visit Mommy's friend, who was sick but is getting better. I want her to meet him, but I'm not ready to explain who he is yet.

I've called ahead to make sure Willa won't be there for a while, and Brad assured me that she'd only come in for a brief time that morning and wouldn't return until after dinner. I also told him that I was bringing Alyssa but didn't want to break the news to her, at least not this time. He seemed okay with that.

We stop in front of the door to the room, and I take a minute to compose myself. There are so many butterflies in my stomach that I'm sure they'll start flying from my ears. This moment is bigger than I expected — she may not know it, but my daughter is about to meet someone who's part of her, forever. It's daunting.

When I don't go in right away, Alyssa looks up at me. "Should we ring the doorbell, Mommy?"

Her innocent question relaxes me, and I laugh and reach for the handle. "They don't have doorbells here, munchkin," I say. "We can just go in."

"Oh, okay. I like doorbells, though."

"Me too," I say with a smile.

I take a breath and push the door open. And my first thought is that something's gone wrong, because the bed and the chair beside it are empty, and the wheelchair is nowhere in evidence. No wheelchair . . . and no Brad.

Then I hear a muted flush from behind the closed bath-room door, and my heart starts to beat again.

144

"Come on, sweetheart. My friend will be here in a minute," I say as I lead my daughter into the room. "We'll just sit down and wait."

Alyssa looks around at everything with thoughtful consideration as we approach the chair next to the bed. I sit down and lift her onto my lap, and she says, "Mommy, is your friend a magician?"

I look at her. "Why would you think that?"

"Because magicians pop out from nowhere," she says. "Like this." She covers her face with her small hands and then throws both arms out. "Ta-dah!"

I hug her and laugh. "I guess you know a lot about magicians," I say. "But no, my friend isn't one of them. He's just in the bathroom, see?" I point to the closed door across the room.

She follows my gesture and nods. "Okay. But it would be cool if he was a magician."

In a way, Brad *is* a magician, and he's pulled off the greatest trick of all: coming back from the dead. But I'm not sure that's an appropriate conversation to have with my four-year-old daughter.

The handle on the bathroom door clicks down, and I hold my breath as the door swings open. It seems to move by itself. Then I realize that there must be one of those handicapped buttons to open the door, because Brad is standing there behind an aluminum-frame walker, smiling out at me.

"I thought I heard voices," he says as he walks slowly into the room, pushing the walker before him. "I wasn't sure if I had visitors, or I was going crazy."

Alyssa giggles. "Your friend is funny, Mommy," she whispers. "I like him."

My heart soars. *She likes him.* It's a definite step in the right direction.

"Let's go say hello," I tell her quietly, and she nods and slides to the floor.

Alyssa is fast, and she reaches Brad almost before I'm fully standing. He stops and stares down at her over the walker, smiling hesitantly.

"Hello," she says, her face turned up in solemn greeting as she lifts a tiny hand toward him. "My name is Alyssa Dawn Bauman."

Brad's features work briefly, and he takes her hand with infinite gentleness. "Hi, Alyssa. I'm Brad," he says with a catch in his voice. "I'm very happy to meet you."

She beams at him. "Hi, Brad. There's a boy in my class named Brad too, only Mrs. Jocasta calls him Brad-*ley* because he always throws the blocks. But I never throw blocks. I think it's mean."

"I think you're right," Brad says hoarsely as he grips the walker again. His hands are shaking, and his eyes are wide and startled. "It *is* mean to throw blocks. You're a very smart girl, Alyssa."

"Thank you," she says. "I like being smart."

I can tell that Brad is nearly overcome with emotion. If he doesn't sit down soon, he might collapse. I close the distance to my daughter and reach down to rub her back. "Hey, munchkin, can you go sit in that chair for a minute?" I say. "If it's okay with Brad, maybe you can turn the television on and see if there's anything interesting."

"She can sit on the bed." Brad flashes a wan smile and nods toward it. "The remote is right there by the pillow. And . . . I think I'm going to need the chair."

"Okay. Thanks, Brad!" Alyssa calls as she runs off and scrambles up the side of the bed. Soon she's working the remote like a pro.

"Celine. Oh, God . . ."

Brad whispers the words, and I turn just as he shoves the walker aside and throws his arms around me. His embrace is firm and trembling. "She's so *tiny*," he rasps, his breath feathering my ear. "Tiny, and perfect."

I hug him back, until he finally stops shaking, and then smile at him. "Do you want me to grab the walker for you?"

"No." He turns his head away and wipes a few stray tears. "Maybe you could help me over there, though? My legs don't seem interested in cooperating."

146

"Of course I will."

I keep an arm around his waist, and he leans on my shoulders as we move toward the chair. When we reach it, he grabs one of the arms and lowers himself in with a long breath. "Phew. Made it," he says. "Thank you."

From his tone, I know he's thanking me for more than helping him walk. I glance at Alyssa and smile. "You're welcome."

This visit won't be so bad, after all.

CHAPTER 25

Jill comes over that night. She looks much better than she sounded yesterday, like she's completely gotten over the cold, and she's happy about her date with Hunter.

What she's not so thrilled about is to hear that I've brought Alyssa to meet Brad.

After I tuck my daughter into bed at eight, since she has school tomorrow, Jill hangs around to talk. She's sitting at the island counter in the kitchen while I make coffee — we've decided to skip the wine because we both have an early day tomorrow. "I'm not sure you should have told him, Celine," she says, toying with her phone on the counter. "Did you forget what a jerk he was before?"

I shake my head as I get two mugs out of the cupboard and set them by the coffee machine while it burbles away. "No, I didn't forget," I say, heading to the fridge for the creamer. "Like I said, though, we were both young. I just . . . if there's a chance that Alyssa can have her father in her life, I want to take it."

Jill rolls her eyes good-naturedly. "You still love him, don't you?"

"Maybe." I don't look at her when I say it.

I fix the coffees, sit at the counter across from her and place a mug on her side. "I didn't get to tell you, the police arrested someone today for Teryn's murder."

"Holy shit, they did?" Jill says. "Tell me it was Hannah."

"No, it was another nurse at the hospital. Kate Engle," I say. "At least, that's their official stance. But not everyone believes it."

She frowns. "What do you mean?"

"Detective Chambers, the guy who's been working this case, thinks it's too convenient." A cloud passes over me as I remember the conversation we had, how he'd been genuinely sorry that he couldn't do anything about it, even though he knew it was all wrong. "They found the same poison in this other nurse's locker that had been used to kill Teryn, but it was five days after her murder. I mean, if you were going to kill someone, would you keep the evidence that you'd done it hanging around in your locker?"

"I don't know. I've never thought about what I'd do if I killed someone before," Jill says with a laugh. But her smile fades, and she says, "So whoever's doing this is still out there?"

"They have to be," I say. "I have no idea who Kate Engle is, but she isn't the one who's been texting me."

"Oh my God, you're right. Did you tell the police that?"

I stare at my coffee. "Unfortunately, the detective made it clear that the case is very closed. They wouldn't do anything about it, even if I did tell them," I say.

"It's Hannah, then," Jill says. "It has to be her."

"Actually, I don't think it is." I tell her about the party last night, about meeting the daughter who hates her and how upset she was about everything. "She's really been through a lot. She explained why things seemed the way they did with her, and it made sense. So I guess there is someone else."

Jill takes a deep breath. "Do you and Alyssa want to stay with me for a while?" she says. "You know . . . just so there's someone else around, and you're not anywhere obvious. I wouldn't mind. I have plenty of room."

I smile at her. "You're so sweet. But don't worry, we'll be okay," I say. "Besides, what if you want to have Hunter over? We'd be in the way."

She blushes faintly. "I haven't decided about that yet. But . . . are you sure? I really wouldn't mind."

"I'm sure."

We finish our coffee and talk for a while, and then Jill stands and stretches, yawning. "Guess it's time to turn in," she says. "I have to be at the office at seven tomorrow, because *Danny* forgot to tell me about yet another filing deadline."

I groan in sympathy. Dan does seem like a nice guy, but he's definitely got a few stereotypical blond traits — like being kind of dumb sometimes. At least he seems to make Missy happy for some reason.

"Just a second. I'll walk you out," I say as I grab the coffee mugs and put them in the sink. "I think I could use a little air."

We head out through the kitchen door to the garage, and I hit the opener to raise the garage entrance. Jill's red Fiat is parked out in the driveway. We walk past my car, and once I step outside the garage, I take a deep breath of cool night air and let it clear my head. There are so many things running through it that I can barely think straight.

"Celine," Jill hisses suddenly, grabbing my arm as she stares down the driveway. "You see that?"

I follow her gaze to a dark-blue sedan parked at the curb across the street, in front of the vacant lot that's been for sale by a rival real estate company for over a year. "It's a car," I say slowly. "Unless I'm missing something?"

"Someone is sitting in the driver's seat," Jill says. "Don't you think that's a little suspicious? Whoever it is, they're hanging out in front of a vacant lot *across from your house*. And you just told me the police aren't looking into the person who's been threatening you anymore."

My gut clenches. "Okay, maybe it is suspicious," I murmur, warily eyeing the sedan and its shadow of a person at the wheel. "I'll just go back inside—"

The hand on my arm squeezes. "You have to call 911!"

I almost do it, but then I realize I'd sound like a crazy person. Hello, operator, I'd like to report a person sitting in a car. They don't send police out for that. "I can't," I tell Jill as I take my phone from my pocket. "But I can call Ollie."

Her brow furrows. "Ollie?"

"Detective Chambers," I explain, pulling up his number. I tap to dial and hold the phone to my ear.

When the first ring sounds, there's a flash of light inside the dark sedan.

"Oh my God, I don't believe it," I murmur, an absent smile tugging at my lips. I watch as the shadowy figure in the car extends an arm toward the light, picks up a cell phone and taps it before lifting it to his head.

"Looks like I'm busted." Ollie's voice fills my ear, deep with wry amusement. "Okay, I'm coming out. Don't shoot."

I laugh. "Don't worry, I'm unarmed."

"What's going on?" Jill says.

"Just look." I hang up the phone and point across the street, where the sedan's door is opening. A figure emerges, steps onto the curb and turns around, raising his hands over his head. There's a phone in one of them, and a big sheepish grin on his face.

He puts his arms down and jogs across the street, and I turn to my astonished friend. "This is Detective Oliver Chambers," I tell her. "Ollie. I think he's trying to protect me or something."

"Well, you're not wrong about that." Ollie is walking up the driveway, shoving his phone in a pocket. "Sorry if I scared you," he says. "I thought about telling you I'd planned to stake out your place, but then I figured it would be weird."

"Yes. It is kind of weird," I say, matching his grin. "Ollie, this is my best friend, Jill Mazer."

"Hello, Jill." He holds a hand out, and she takes it with an open-mouthed stare. "Is this your car?"

"Um, yes," she stammers. "Hello."

"Good. I guess I won't have to run your plates, after all," he says with a teasing smile, and then releases her hand to take mine. "Ms. Bauman. It's good to see you again."

"Celine, remember?" I have to restrain a sudden urge to hug him. I'm absurdly touched that he's here on his own time, trying to watch out for me. "Even though you're stalking me, it's good to see you, too."

He laughs and rubs the back of his neck. "Well, if you don't mind, I might hang around and stalk you a little more," he says. "I'm still not convinced that you're safe."

"I won't say no. That is, if it's not putting you out," I say. "You don't have to do this for me, you know."

The slanted smile he gives me sends my heart into overdrive. "I want to."

"Okay, then." My mouth has gone a little dry. "Thank you, Ollie."

He grins again, sketches a little salute, and then jogs back to his car.

"Holy shit, he's hot," Jill says once the sedan door is shut with Ollie inside. "Like, *really* hot."

I nod absently. "Is he? I hadn't noticed."

I'm lying, to myself as much as Jill. I definitely noticed the way his t-shirt clings to his muscles, the strong lines of his face, those deep blue, penetrating eyes that look a whole lot sexier when they're not interrogating me with silent questions. And his ass in those jeans. Damn, I might need to go fan myself for a while.

If I wasn't in love with Brad, I could easily see myself falling for Detective Oliver Chambers.

CHAPTER 26

I'm at the office, and both Maxine and Sabrina are treating me with a kind of skittish awe. Lucas missed my little display of dominance on Friday and probably has no idea what's going on, but he seems to be amused at the way they're so jumpy around me.

The police have returned my computer, totally scrubbed, and I'm spending the morning re-installing programs and restoring my files from the backup cloud server. The first showing for my new luxury listing is scheduled for noon, and Hannah's going with me to get a little experience. She's decided not to give up on real estate the way she's given up on everything else she's tried.

I think it's a strange career choice for someone who's independently wealthy, but if she really likes it, I guess it won't hurt.

At around 9:30, my replacement cell phone rings, and Hannah's number shows on the screen. At least this time I'm not worried about answering it. I pick up and say, "Hey, did you change your mind about today already?"

Hannah laughs. "Nope. I'm not flaking out this time," she says. "But I wanted to tell you something exciting, at least for me. I hope you don't mind."

"Mind what?"

"Er. That I'm telling you about it," she says. "I'm sorry. That came out wrong."

I smile. "It's okay, I get it now. You can just tell me stuff."

"Okay." She takes a deep breath. "You'll never guess where I am right now. At the elementary school," she says without waiting for me to guess. "Izzy's class is having a Parent Day, and she asked me to come instead of Julie."

"Oh, Hannah. That's wonderful!" I say, my eyes misting over a little for her. "Listen, you don't have to come to the showing today. If your daughter wants you there, you should stay with her."

"Well, the Parent Day thing isn't supposed to take long," she says. "I can just meet you at the house, if that's okay? I have the address."

"Sure, that's fine. I'll see you then," I tell her. "And really, don't worry if you can't make it. Izzy is way more important."

"I agree. Thank you, Celine."

I smile as I hang up, glad that something's going right for Hannah. I do hope she's able to mend her relationship with her daughter, after all her family has been through. That poor little girl will never know her grandparents, and Hannah won't have any parental advice to help her through tough times. Not that all advice parents offer to their grown children is good — if I'd followed my mother's advice, I'd be stuck in some high-powered, high-pressure career with no time for my daughter.

Vaguely, I wonder who Izzy's father is, but it doesn't really matter. Hannah's never mentioned him, which probably means he's out of the picture.

Not a minute after I set my phone on the desk, it chimes with a text notification. A brief pulse of dread moves through me as I pick it up again to look, but the text is from Hannah. And there's an attachment, a photo.

I tap the image to open it, and my phone's screen goes black.

"What the . . ." I murmur, reaching for the power button. But just then it flashes back to life, and an image fills the

154

screen. Alyssa and Izzy, standing in the hallway at the school beneath a bulletin board hung with kindergarten drawings. Their arms are slung around each other's shoulders, and they're both grinning like crazy.

Hannah's message appears beneath the photo: *Best friends. Aren't they adorable? Thought you might like a copy of this.*

I smile and trace a finger across my daughter's smile, and then close the image. Later tonight, I'll transfer it to my home computer where I've been saving all my pictures.

There's still a few hours before the showing, so I get back to rebuilding my computer. I've just started downloading some of my files from the cloud to the hard drive when the extension light on my desk phone flashes, accompanied by a strident buzz. Oh, good. Courtney transferred a call to me from the front desk. Probably one she couldn't be bothered to handle herself.

I pick up the handset and press the flashing button. "Hughes Real Estate, this is Celine," I say.

"Hey, Celine. It's Brad."

My brow furrows. He sounds exhausted, maybe even sad, and I'm not sure why he called the office instead of my phone. "Hey. Is everything okay?"

"Yeah, I just . . ." He gives a ragged sigh. "I'm sorry for calling you at work, but I don't have your number," he says.

I almost slap my forehead. Of course he doesn't have my cell — I never gave it to him, and I've only talked to him on the hospital room phone. Those don't come with caller ID. "It's no problem. What's up?"

He hesitates and then says, "I need to talk to you, but I don't want to do it on the phone. Can you come to the hospital for a minute?"

I'm getting a little worried. He sounds more miserable with every word. I can think of a dozen things that might've gone wrong — he's changed his mind about Alyssa, or me. His mother had a meltdown. His doctor told him that he's going to have long-term problems. "Okay. I do have some time before my next appointment," I say. "Can I get a hint about what's wrong?"

"I'd rather tell you in person," he whispers hoarsely.

Oh, no. It must be really bad. "All right, I'll be there in a few minutes," I say.

"Thank you, Celine."

As I hang up, I'm already grabbing my purse and briefcase. I shove my phone in my pocket and hurry toward the back door, ignoring the look from Sabrina.

Something strange occurs to me while I'm getting in the car. Brad just called the office number to reach me . . . but I never told him where I worked or what I did. At least, I can't recall telling him. But it's easy enough to look me up online, since my name shows up on a lot of listings. That must be what he did.

I start the engine and head for the hospital, hoping that whatever Brad wants to talk about isn't as bad as I think it is.

CHAPTER 27

Willa Dowling is in the house when I walk into Brad's room, and she looks twice as pissed as the last time. The instant she sees me, her face flushes brick red and she opens her mouth to scream.

"Mother, don't," Brad says sharply from the bed. His head is inclined, but he's lying limp beneath a sheet pulled to his waist, and the hollows under his eyes are darker than ever. "Please, just go to the cafeteria and get a cup of coffee, or something. I need a few minutes."

Willa rounds on him, sputtering with a hand in the air. He shoots her a glare, and she whirls and stalks past me, bumping my shoulder hard on the way.

Once she's out of the room, Brad groans softly and closes his eyes. "I wish she'd stop doing that," he says, shaking his head. He looks at me and gulps, then gestures to the chair beside him. "You should probably sit down for this."

My jaw clenches with anticipation as I cross the room and take a seat. "What is it?" I say. "You're having health problems, aren't you? Complications from the coma."

He smirks. "You know, I actually wish that was it," he says. "But no. I have to talk to you about . . . that night. The accident. And it's kind of a long story, so you'll have to bear with me, okay?"

"All right," I whisper. Now I have no idea what to expect, but from the look on his face, I know it can't be good.

Brad looks away and composes himself, and then folds his hands in his lap. "Before I tell you this, I want you to know that I'm so glad you let me meet Alyssa," he says. "She really is amazing. And . . . I'm afraid I'm not worthy to be in her life, or yours."

That isn't on the list of things I might have expected. "What do you mean? Of course you are," I say. "You're her father."

"No I'm not. Worthy, I mean." His chest heaves once. "First, I need to tell you why I left," he says. "You asked about our future, whether we'd stay together, and I panicked. I have serious commitment issues, thanks to all that time with Hannah." Anger darkens his green eyes for a moment. "You can probably imagine why, but after her, I never wanted to be tied down to one person again. At least, I thought I didn't."

"Yes, I think I can imagine." I don't tell him what Hannah said to me, about how sorry she is for the way she treated him. If there's going to be an apology there, it'll have to come from her. "So you thought you didn't . . . ?" I prompt.

He nods slowly. "I was wrong about that. I loved you . . . I still love you," he says, shivering slightly. "And I *did* want to commit. But I was so terrified to tell you the truth, to open up that way, that I ran instead. But . . ." He winces and looks away. "But I didn't go to a liquor store. I went to Monkey Shines."

The off-campus bar. "Okay," I say carefully. "So you got drunk there, instead of in your car or whatever."

"Yes. But I didn't get drunk alone." He stares intently at his hands, squeezing them until his knuckles tighten. "Jill was there."

I blink. "Jill Mazer?"

"She was your best friend," he says quickly. "I thought if I talked to her, maybe . . . I don't know. I had some idea of making you see reason, understand why I couldn't commit, so you wouldn't leave me. I thought you'd break up with me if I said no. And Jill said she'd listen, and she started buying me drinks." He tips his head back to stare at the ceiling. "A lot of drinks."

Oh, my God. "Jill got you drunk," I say. "And she let you *drive* after that?"

"She didn't just get me drunk." He finally looks at me, with bright tears standing in his eyes. "She was flirting with me the whole time. I was plastered and upset about you, and I just . . . well, I didn't turn her down."

"You . . ." I manage before my throat closes around the rest. My stomach heaves, and I wrap my arms around my midsection to keep from throwing up. "You slept with her."

He nods miserably. "In the bathroom at Monkey Shines," he says. "It was stupid and terrible, and part of me knew that, but I still went ahead and did it. *That's* why I'm not worthy," he whispers. "Because I did that to you."

My head pounds with blinding force. Jill got drunk with Brad, and *screwed him in the bathroom*, right before the accident. All this time she'd told me what a piece of shit he is, reminded me how terribly he'd treated me, but she never mentioned why.

This is why. I can't believe she'd not only do this to me, but keep being my friend all these years, acting like it never happened.

No wonder she was so upset when I told him about Alyssa.

"Celine?" Brad sounds like he's just lost ten years of his life in five minutes. "God, I'm so sorry. I'll never be able to apologize enough."

I'm not sure how to respond to that, so I don't.

"What really freaks me out about the whole thing is what she said to me . . . after," Brad says in a pained tone. "It was so bizarre. I'll never forget it."

I force myself to look at him. "What did she say?"

"She . . ." He coughs to clear his throat. "She said, 'I knew you'd pick me over her. I have it all planned out. When the time comes, she won't be a problem.'"

My breath whooshes out of me. The murders, the frame jobs, the texts.

It was Jill.

"I have to go," I say, springing to my feet. "Wait . . . Brad, has Jill been here to see you?"

He looks extremely uncomfortable. "She was here Friday night," he admits. "Talking crazy about how we were going to be together soon. I told her to leave . . ."

Friday night. When she told me she had a date with that Hunter guy. That's why she had a bug the next day — she must've picked it up from someone at the hospital.

And she'd probably planted the poison in Kate Engle's locker while she was here.

"Okay, thank you," I say, and head for the door.

"Does this mean you don't want to see me anymore?" Brad calls miserably. "I wouldn't blame you if you don't."

I turn briefly to look at him. I can't make this decision right now, so I hedge. "Mostly I'm angry with Jill for not telling me what happened that night," I say. "She should have, because you couldn't. But I really have to go right now."

He nods. "I understand."

No, he really doesn't. And I don't have time to explain.

I practically run for the elevators, pulling my phone out on the way. Once I'm inside headed for the parking garage level, I dial Ollie's number. But the phone doesn't ring. There's nothing but silence.

Frowning, I try again. The same thing happens.

"What is *wrong* with you?" I shout at the phone, just as the elevator dings and the doors open to a startled man in a suit who must've heard me yelling. "Sorry. My phone's not working," I mumble as I brush past him.

I need to get a hold of Ollie, right now, so I head further into the hospital instead of toward the parking garage. There's an information desk in the hallway with a woman sitting behind it, and I step up to the desk attempting to look like a calm, controlled person. "Hi," I say. "My cell phone just died, and I'm having a little emergency here. By any chance is there a phone here somewhere I could use?"

The receptionist hesitates, and then picks up the receiver of the desk phone and hands it to me. "If you'll tell me the number you're calling, I can dial it for you," she says.

"Thank you so much." I prop the receiver on my shoulder, find Ollie's number on my phone and read it off to her. She punches an extension line and presses the numbers, and I wait through three rings that seem to take a very long time before he answers.

"Ollie, it's Celine," I say quickly. "I know who's behind everything. Can you meet me at my house?"

"I'm on the way," he says with no hesitation.

"Thank you."

Relief fills me as I hand the phone back to the receptionist. I thank her again and rush off to the parking garage. I can be home in ten minutes from here, and I hope Ollie gets there soon.

Because the first thing I need to do is find Jill.

CHAPTER 28

Ollie isn't there yet when I get home. I pull into the garage, leaving the door open, and get the stupid, broken phone out to try calling Jill. But nothing happens on the other end. No ringing, no error message, nothing. So I try to send her a text.

I get a Can't Send notification with a nice red exclamation point.

Frustrated and on the verge of terrified, I nearly throw the phone across the garage. But I think better of it, pocketing it instead as I walk up the stairs and open the door to the kitchen. I don't have a house phone — never thought I needed one. At this moment I'm regretting that decision.

I'll just have to borrow Ollie's when he gets here.

I hunt through the fridge for a cold drink and find a lone bottle of water. Good enough. I twist the cap off and swallow a third of it without stopping, though it barely takes the edge off. My throat aches with strain and dry fear, and I'm not sure I can talk in a normal voice.

Right now, it's a little before noon. Almost three hours until Alyssa gets out of school. With a bit of luck, I'm hoping that all this will be over and Ollie will have arrested Jill before I pick up my daughter. At least she's safely away from the insanity.

As I drink more water, I hear sirens in the distance and manage a small smile. Whatever Ollie had been doing when I called him, he must've dropped it fast. I head out of the kitchen and through the garage, planning to meet him outside and go from there.

I'm in the driveway when the police car screeches to the curb, lights flashing and siren wailing. The siren turns off, but the lights stay on as both front doors open and Detective Garfield emerges from the passenger side, while Ollie gets out of the driver's seat. I start toward them.

And I freeze when the phone in my pocket chimes. The one that doesn't work.

The detectives are moving fast, already asking questions, but I barely hear them. I slide the phone out and see the little 1 on the text message bubble. Maybe the text I sent Jill went through after all, and this is her reply.

I open the message, and a silent scream lodges in my throat.

You shouldn't have told him about Alyssa. Now you'll never see her again.

"No!" I shout hoarsely, desperately tapping the message as if I can make it go away, make it never happen. I don't realize that I'm shaking until big, warm hands wrap around mine and squeeze gently.

"Celine." Ollie's blue eyes are dark with concern. "What is it?"

"Your phone. I need your phone, please. Right now," I rasp.

He gives it to me without question, and then takes mine. I dial 411, knowing there's no way I'll be able to focus enough to look up the school's number and dial it. Dimly, I'm aware of Ollie reading the text that's still on the screen, of horror washing over his face as he tears the CB unit from his belt and starts shouting instructions into it.

The directory assistance system picks up, and I wait until I'm asked what number I want to reach. "Wolfsbrook Elementary School," I say, and wait again. The automated voice reads off the number and asks me if I'd like to be connected.

"Yes," I say frantically.

It seems to take forever, but finally the phone rings twice, and a pleasant woman's voice answers. "Wolfsbrook Elementary."

"This is Celine Bauman," I say, with no attempt to be polite. "My daughter Alyssa is in Mrs. Jocasta's class, and I need to come and get her right now. Can you bring her to the office or something?"

"Oh, Mrs. Bauman, I'm so glad you called," the woman says. "I tried to reach you earlier this morning, but there was no answer. Alyssa had a very upset tummy."

"Had?" I blurt. "Where is she?"

I must sound a lot angrier than I meant to, because the woman gasps. "Well, she was really quite sick, vomiting," the woman stammers. "And we couldn't reach you, so we called her emergency contact to have her picked up." She pauses as if she's looking for something, and then says, "Jill Mazer. She came to get Alyssa about an hour ago."

A violent contortion grips my entire body, and the phone falls from my hands onto the driveway. It bounces on the rubber case and lands face-up. A small, tinny voice drifts up from the phone as the woman keeps talking, but I no longer care what she has to say.

Jill has her. She has my daughter.

Alyssa is not safe.

* * *

I can finally breathe a little, but I'm not sure it's going to last long.

Ollie is sitting in my living room with me. There are two cups of takeout coffee on the table, his nearly gone and mine virtually untouched. I tried to drink some of it, but it settled like ashes in my mouth.

The only reason I'm breathing is that I'm numb. I've screamed and cried myself completely out.

While I was calling about Alyssa, Ollie read the text and had immediately dispatched officers to the elementary school. He ended up calling them off before they got there, when I told him she was gone. Somehow I got through telling him Jill's home address and where she worked, even though I knew she wouldn't be at either of those places.

She wasn't.

The police are searching for her right now. They have photos of her and Alyssa from my computer, and a description of her car and the license plate number has been sent to both the county and state police along with the photos.

Three hours. My daughter has been missing for three hours now, and I have no idea why Jill took her or where she went. She could've made it out of New Hampshire already.

Oh, God, I can't think about that. I'm going to be sick again.

Detective Garfield took my malfunctioning phone to the police lab, so they could try to find out something from it, and is coming back with yet another replacement phone for me to use. Ollie stayed here to wait for him. He doesn't want to leave me alone, but I know he'll have to soon. He's got a job to do.

He has to find my daughter.

"Do you know what the worst thing is?" I say, noticing the horrible, hollow drag in my voice but unable to do anything about it. "She *knows* Jill. Alyssa might not even think anything is wrong right now, wherever she is. She'll think I'm coming to get her eventually, until . . . until I don't," I whisper. "Oh, God. Why did she take my baby?"

Ollie seizes my hand. "We're going to find her. I swear we will."

I want to believe that, desperately. But I'm too stunned to feel much of anything, especially hope.

"I can't do this," I gasp suddenly, leaning forward in an attempt to stand. "I can't sit here and . . . and wait for . . . I *have* to get my daughter."

I'm on my feet, turning toward the dining room, when Ollie grabs my arm and turns me around. "Celine, there's nothing you can do," he says firmly. "I know how awful that is to hear—"

"No, you don't," I snap at him. "Do you have any kids?"

He grimaces. "No. But I'm telling you that rushing off to God knows where isn't going to help you, or Alyssa." His hands move to my shoulders, gently restraining me. "I've got every resource out there looking for your daughter. And if you go, there won't be anyone to protect *you*."

"I don't want to be protected!" My voice crackles, and another round of tears fill my eyes. "I don't care what happens to me. All that matters is Alyssa."

"*I* care what happens," he says, staring into my eyes. "We will find her."

His concerned look breaks me, and I fall against him, sobbing.

Ollie wraps his arms around me, a warm and protective circle. He feels good, safe, and even though it comforts me, I hate it. I hate being secure in my house, surrounded by law enforcement, while my daughter is out there somewhere for reasons I don't understand, and her life may be in danger.

I don't know what Jill wants with her. That's the real agony of it.

I'm still leaning on Ollie when the doorbell rings, and he lifts my chin tenderly to look at me. "That's Pete. Detective Garfield," he says. "Why don't you sit down, and I'll let him in?"

I sniffle and nod, and he leads me to the couch and helps me down before he goes to answer the door. A minute later he's back with a cell phone in his hand, just a cheap throwaway. "It's not your number, but it's activated," he says. "I need to keep in touch with you. I'm going to put the number for this phone in mine, okay?"

"Sure," I say with a shrug.

He messes with both phones for a few minutes, and then hands the new one to me. "My number's in there," he says. "And I'm so sorry, but we have to go for a while. I'm not leaving you alone, though. There's a squad car with two officers out front, and we'll have a constant presence here with you until we find Alyssa."

My throat clenches, and I'm grateful that he said *until*. "All right. Thank you," I say. "I guess I'll . . . be here."

I might not be for long, but I won't tell him that. I haven't decided fully myself. I'll try to stay here and stay safe, try to wait and let the police do their job, but I can't guarantee it will work out that way.

My daughter isn't safe, and I need her to be. That's *my* job.

Ollie rubs my shoulder and reminds me to call him if I need anything, and then he and his partner leave. I stay where I am for a few minutes, and when I hear a car engine start outside and a vehicle drive away, I get up and walk into the kitchen. So I'm near the exit.

Now that I have a working phone to myself, I dial Jill's number. It rings once and goes to an automated message about the person I'm trying to call not being available. I didn't really expect her to answer, anyway. Still, I compose a text to her number.

If you hurt my daughter, I'll kill you.

I send the message without a second thought, and then sit at the island counter and try to breathe. Try to think. I have to do something, I just *have* to. But what? If I was Jill, where would I go with Alyssa?

And why would I take her in the first place?

No answers come to me. I sit for a few more minutes, and decide that maybe I'll call Hannah. I'm not sure I could even tell her what happened without breaking down and probably being unable to continue, but at least she might understand how I feel. She has a daughter, too.

Plus, I never did anything about cancelling or rescheduling the showing. She might be worried about me if she went there and I didn't show up.

I dial her number and wait. It rings several times, and then her voicemail picks up, but I can't bring myself to leave a message. I don't know what I'll say. I hang up and think vaguely that I'll try again later.

That's when the new phone dings with a text message. It's from Jill.

If you want your daughter back, come to Bronmeyer Park tonight at ten. Come alone. Do not tell the police, or she dies.

My heart freezes, and a new spark forms deep in my gut. It's pure rage. I consider telling Ollie about the message for all of five seconds, but I refuse to risk my daughter's life for any reason. I know Bronmeyer Park — it's about a block away from the Quintaine property, Hannah's new house. I can't imagine why Jill wants to meet there, but it doesn't matter. I absolutely meant what I said. If she hurts my daughter, I'll kill her.

I tap the reply box, type out a message, and hit send.

I'll be there.

CHAPTER 29

Waiting around to confront the woman who's stolen my daughter is agony.

I've talked to Ollie at least four times since I got Jill's text. I haven't told him about it, even though I want to. He's grown steadily more exhausted every time we've spoken, and I know he's running himself ragged trying to find my daughter.

I wish I could tell him. But the risk is too big. I won't lose her.

He calls again around nine. When I answer the phone, he says, "No news yet. Just checking in. How are you holding up?"

"Still breathing." It's the same thing I've told him every time. It's all I *can* do — at least until ten o'clock. One more slow, torturous hour. "What about you?"

"Same here," he says. "Listen, I know it probably seems like nothing is happening, but we've pulled out all the stops. And we're still well within the critical time frame for . . ."

When he doesn't continue, I say, "Finding kidnapped children?"

"Missing persons," he says. He's been trying to get me not to use the K-word. "Celine, have you eaten anything at all today?"

169

The question is so unexpected that I laugh, and it startles me. I sound like a maniac. "Come to think of it, no. I haven't," I say.

"Well, tell me what you want. Anything, and I'll have it delivered to you," he says. "You have to try and keep your strength up."

That's probably a good point. But I don't want an extra police officer or two showing up here with dinner while I'm trying to sneak out of the house without them noticing. "Tell you what. I've got plenty of food here, and I promise I'll make something right now and eat. Deal?"

"Are you sure you want to cook? I really don't mind getting something sent over."

I open the fridge and look. "There's sandwich stuff. So I won't have to cook," I say.

"And you're really going to eat."

"Yep. Right now." I'm already pulling bread and lunchmeat out, placing it on the counter. I want to keep my strength up, but not for the reason he thinks.

I may have to overpower Jill.

"Okay. You'd better be," he says. "Can I do anything else for you?"

God, why does he have to be so thoughtful and concerned? It's killing me that I can't tell him about Jill's message. But if something happens to me and Alyssa . . . well, maybe I can drop a hint, and maybe he'll be able to pick it up. Or not.

I'll try anyway.

"You know, I've tried to call Hannah a few times today, but she isn't answering her phone," I say. "I'm a little worried about her. I might go over there later, just to check on things."

There's no way I can work the park into anything, but at least it's near Hannah's house. Maybe if I don't come back, he'll be able to look in the right area. At least I know that if I make it out of here, it won't be long before Ollie realizes I'm gone and starts trying to find me.

"Absolutely not. You can't go anywhere," he says. "Don't worry about Hannah, or anyone else except yourself. It's not safe for you."

I can't help smiling at the stern worry in his voice. "All right. I'll stay here," I tell him. "And I'll eat this sandwich I just made."

"You do that."

He says he has to make more calls, so we hang up. I know he'll check in with me again soon — and next time, I might not be able to answer. The idea terrifies me, but I'm determined to go through with this.

I eat the sandwich and then make a second one and force it down too. By then I think enough time must have passed for me to go and get my daughter, but it's only 9:15. I still have to wait.

Suddenly I realize that there's one more person I should talk to about this, and I haven't even thought of him once in all this time.

Brad is her father. He should know that his daughter is missing.

I have to get the scrap of paper with his room number on it out of my purse, since it was in the memory of my previous phone. I send the call through, and it rings and rings and rings. There's no answer, and no voicemail or 'unavailable' message. Maybe he's sleeping.

But a deep, cold feeling in my gut says I'd better make sure.

I dial information and get connected to the main hospital number, and then ask for the fifth-floor nurses' station. The woman who answers the phone sounds irritated, and I know she's not going to volunteer much help.

So I'll have to make her.

"I need to speak to Brad Dowling right away, and he's not answering the phone in his room," I say after the terse greeting. "Can you go in there and get him for me?"

"Who is this?" the woman says, and then adds, "Never mind. He's probably sleeping, and we don't wake up sleeping patients to take phone calls. This is a hospital."

"He's not sleeping. He's missing."

"Excuse me?"

Speaking the words out loud make me certain of it. "I said, he's missing!" I shout. "Go in his room and check. He's not there."

"This is ridiculous," the woman says, and there's a clunk. But I can still hear the background noises in the hospital. She hasn't hung up the phone — she's just put it on the desk, and hopefully gone to check on Brad.

The few minutes she's gone are endless. When the woman finally returns to the phone, she says angrily, "How did you know that? Who is this? I'm calling the police, right now."

"You do that," I say, and hang up. I'm shaking again. But I make myself stop. Now more than ever, I need to be calm and in control. I've suddenly realized why Jill wants my daughter. Because she's *Brad's* daughter. And now she has him, too.

She's taking my family and giving it to herself.

I can't wait one moment longer. I grab a hoodie from the hook beside the kitchen door, slip it on, and move into the garage. There's a back door leading to the yard, and I go through it and run across the grass, cutting across the neighbor's lawn behind my house to the next block. My heart smashes like it's being pounded hard on an anvil, but I don't stop.

The park is just a little too far away to walk there in time. So I head for the convenience store on the next corner and call for an Uber. I'm told that a car will be there in fifteen minutes, and I ask them to please hurry. They say they'll try.

My ride gets to the convenience store in twelve minutes. I pay almost no attention to the driver as I get in and give the address of the park. I'm watching the phone the whole time, watching the minutes tick closer to my daughter.

It's 9:50 when the Uber car stops in front of the park, which is nothing but a green, grassy expanse with a small clustered playground near the back, bordered by a fringe of trees. I tip the driver extra and get out, rushing across the shaggy, late-fall grass toward the playground. That's the most likely place for Jill to meet me. She wouldn't want to do this out in the open.

I stand by the swing set and wait, facing the street and listening to the neighborhood winding down. The steady sound of crickets overlaid by a brisk, steady autumn wind, and the creak and rustle of the trees as the branches blow. The faint, constant hum of streetlights and the louder, intermittent hum of tires from passing cars. The babble of someone's television through an open window, and someone shouting in the distance. If I squint, I'm pretty sure I can see lights that belong to Hannah's house from here.

Time crawls toward ten o'clock and then past it to 10:01, then 10:02 and 10:03. By ten after, I'm almost too horrified to move and thinking about calling Ollie anyway. She's not here. Something must have happened.

Just then I hear something behind me. A rustling sound like the trees, but closer. Before I can turn to look, there's a huge, hollow *thunk*, and pain explodes in my head, bringing total blackness with it.

CHAPTER 30

I open my eyes with a gasp, but it's still just as dark as it was when I passed out. There isn't a drop of light anywhere, and my head is pounding. I can feel something sticky and wet on the back of my neck that has to be blood. It takes a minute, but I piece together what happened.

Jill hit me with something, knocked me out, and took me . . . somewhere.

Moving is slow and painful, but I can't stay here and do nothing. I feel around with my hands, find that I'm lying on a cold, flat surface — smooth concrete, I think. Is this a garage? The air is cool, slightly musty, but I don't smell anything oily or metallic. This is more of a basement scent, like mildew waiting to happen.

Spending countless hours in hundreds of houses over the years has apparently taught me a few things I never realized I'd learned.

I pat my pockets, hoping to find the phone but knowing I won't, and I'm right. It's gone. I can't see a thing, and I don't hear a sound other than a very faint hum that could be anything, coming from anywhere. I push myself carefully into a seated position and sprawl out with my palms pressed to the floor, taking shallow breaths as dizziness threatens to overcome me. The feeling is slow to fade.

Someone laughs in the darkness.

"Jill?" I call out, suddenly feeling much more in control of myself. Fear and adrenaline has a tendency to drown out everything else. "Damn it, where is Alyssa?"

"Wouldn't you like to know?"

The mocking echo of the text she sent to me, one of the first ones, burns through my blood, and I'm up like a shot and swinging blindly in the dark. "I swear to God, I'll kill you if she's hurt," I growl. "What's wrong with you? How could you do this? You were my *friend*!"

There's a faint click, and a blinding flood of light fills the space around me. I gasp and squint as my head starts pounding again, and my vision gradually adjusts. This is definitely a basement. Poured concrete floor, cement block walls with bleach-white grout . . . a brass-lantern style glass light fixture in the center of the ceiling.

I recognize that light fixture. I've seen it dozens of times over the two years I'd been trying to sell this place.

Why am I in Hannah's house?

"Over here, Celine," Jill calls.

I swing my aching head toward her voice and blink her into focus. She's standing in the entrance to this simple, square room, a 'bonus room' at the back of the expansive basement in the Quintaine property. She has something in her hand, something shiny and metallic and sharp.

A butcher knife.

"This is honestly a shame," Jill says casually as I stand there staring at her. "I was getting better, I really was. I'd just about forgiven you for stealing Brad from me—"

"*From* you?" I rasp, incredulous. "He wasn't *with* you!"

"Shut up and listen," she snaps. "I was going to let it all go. You had Alyssa, and she's part of Brad, but I was happy to let you raise her so I could be the fun one. The surrogate aunt." She takes a menacing step forward. "But then Brad woke up . . . and I knew I had to have it all."

I shudder. "You killed Rosalie. And Teryn."

"Of course I did." She grins and points the knife at me. "*Your* friends. I would've stopped with Rosalie if the cops had actually arrested you like I'd planned, but they didn't. So I moved on to Teryn. And somehow, you weaseled out of that one, too." She shakes her head and sucks her teeth. "I bet you slept with Detective Chambers, didn't you? That's why he let you go. So I had to frame someone else instead."

"He doesn't believe it," I say weakly. "It was too obvious. He's going to keep looking into it."

Jill flaps a hand. "All part of the plan," she says. "We did that on purpose. Soon enough, that detective will find out it was *your* stupid plan to plant the obvious evidence and make the murders look unconnected, to throw them off the trail." Her smile returns, cold and calculating. "It'll be in your suicide note. Then I can tell Alyssa that her mommy was a murderer, and she's better off with me and her daddy."

Out of that whole insane, rambling mess, my mind seizes on a single word. "We?"

"Oh, that's right. Didn't I tell you?" she laughs. "Me and Hannah."

My legs sag in shock, and it takes every ounce of my flagging strength to stay on my feet. At least that explains why I'm here.

"It was brilliant, really, the two of us working together," she says. "She took care of the technical stuff, and I took care of taking your life apart piece by piece. We *both* had you fooled." She gestures with the knife, its flashing arc leaving a streak of light in the air. "It was so *easy* to get Alyssa, too. Hannah visits Izzy at school and slips your daughter a snack with a little ipecac syrup in it, then texts you a picture with an attached virus that shuts down your phone's call function. Alyssa gets sick, the school can't reach Mommy dearest, so they call reliable Aunt Jill, who comes to pick her up. No questions, no suspicion."

I can't bring myself to mention my daughter to this lunatic I thought was my friend, half afraid that just speaking her name will doom her. So I croak, "What about Brad?"

"Oh, we're just going to share. We each get a daughter, and we both get him."

Jesus. If they'd told Brad this insane plan of theirs, he was probably just as terrified as me right now.

I'm trying desperately to figure out a way past Jill when another voice speaks from the gloom behind her. "You know, Jill, I've changed my mind," Hannah says. "I'm not going to share Brad with you, after all."

Jill opens her mouth, starts to turn, and a deafening blast roars through the basement. A deep red stain blossoms at the front of Jill's light blue shirt, spreading rapidly until it soaks her chest. She coughs, and blood foams and oozes from her mouth.

Then she collapses to the ground with a sickening thud.

CHAPTER 31

Without giving myself time to think, I rush for the knife in Jill's outstretched hand. But Hannah is there instantly, pointing the gun she's just used to murder Jill at my head. "I wouldn't do that," she says. "I'm not opposed to killing you slowly."

I glare at her and raise my hands. "Brad was right about you. You're psychotic."

She laughs hard enough to shake her shoulders. "Maybe I am," she says. "And speaking of Brad, you're so distraught over losing him that you're going to kill yourself, after taking your friend with you. It's going to be a murder-suicide." A grin splits her face. "Of course, the police know that Jill took your daughter, and Brad. That's why I sent her to the hospital. They'll never find them where I'm going to stash them. And then once the heat dies down and they stop looking, I'll just quietly leave town and join my family. Rich people do eccentric things all the time."

The whole time she's talking, I'm edging toward Jill's body, trying to reach the knife. She finally notices and fires the gun at the floor, a few feet away from me. The bullet ricochets and slices across my upper arm, drawing a stream of blood that soaks my shirt and hoodie.

"Don't even think about it," Hannah says.

"Why?" I say angrily. "You're just going to kill me anyway."

"Yes, I am. But if you try to fight it, I'm going to kill Alyssa too," she says with a sneer. "I didn't even want your cheerful little brat of a daughter. I was going to get rid of her, but my Izzy wants a friend. And it's like you said to me earlier . . . Izzy is way more important."

Hearing her twist the words I spoke in kindness and spit them back at me is the last straw. Absolute rage explodes through every fiber of my being, and I lunge at her.

She's too surprised to bring the gun up fast enough. She pulls the trigger anyway, but the shot misses and I'm on her, knocking her to the ground. I grab a handful of platinum-blond hair and slam the back of her skull against the hard basement floor, again and again, until her struggles weaken and she stops moving.

Then I wrench the gun from her stiff hand and start across the basement toward the stairs. I know this house like the back of my hand.

And I'm going to find my daughter.

* * *

Alyssa has to be here somewhere, her and Brad both. Hannah said that the police would never find them where she was *going* to stash them, which meant that she hadn't stashed them yet. So they're in the house, somewhere.

I refuse to believe otherwise.

I'm trying to hurry and keep it quiet at the same time. There's still Julie to consider. She works for Hannah, and I can't be sure that she isn't on the side of the crazy lady who pays her. As for Izzy . . . I shudder to think of what's happening to her right now. She's only four, like Alyssa. She can't possibly go along with this willingly.

No wonder the poor child hates her mother. She probably senses that she's psychotic.

The basement stairs lead to an alcove-slash-pantry at the back of the smaller of the two kitchens on the ground floor. I know the door creaks slightly, so I grip the gun tight in one hand and slowly push the door open with the other. There's no sound from the other side, and only a dim light shining from the kitchen, but it's enough to reveal that no one's standing in the pantry.

My first instinct is to find a phone and call Ollie, or 911. But I know there's no house phone here, and I didn't have time to search Jill and find out whether she had mine on her.

I'm not sure whether Hannah is dead, or just unconscious. In case she's the latter, I have to find them before she wakes up.

I step out of the basement and peer into the kitchen. Looks empty. This is the back of the house, so I'll work my way to the front room by room, and if I don't find anything, I'll take the stairs near the front door to the second floor. There's also a full attic. I'm hoping to find them before I have to go up there.

No one is in the formal dining room, the big ultra-modern kitchen, the study, or the den. That leaves the living room and the parlor on the first floor. I check the parlor first, since the entrance is closer than the archway leading to the living room.

And this time I find something. An indistinct shape lying on the floor by the Chesterfield where I'd stupidly tried to comfort poor, lying, viciously calculating Hannah. The light isn't on in the room and I don't dare turn it on. There's just enough backlight from the foyer to make out the size of the shape — much too big to be a four-year-old. It's an adult, possibly Brad.

The shape doesn't seem to be breathing.

I creep-rush toward the shape and crouch down, trying to keep my body out of the dim patch of light from the foyer. This is definitely a person, but it's not Brad. It's Julie. She's face-down on the carpet, her blond hair sprawled messily around her head, but there's something wrong with it. The shadows on her hair are all wrong.

I shake her shoulder gently. It's unpleasantly stiff. Swallowing a lump of nausea, I attempt to roll her over, and move her far enough to see the bloody hole in the center of her forehead, where she'd been shot.

A startled cry surges through me, and I let go of the body to clap my hand over my mouth and muffle it. She's the only one I was worried might hear me, but it feels wrong to scream here in the company of the dead. And Hannah might hear it, if she's only unconscious and I'm loud enough.

I straighten and head for the living room. At first I think there's no one in here either, but then I see the curve of a head at the top of a wingback chair that faces the fireplace. Whoever it is has dark hair, and I hope it's Brad. I hope he's alive.

Not wanting to give myself away in case it's not Brad, I approach the chair as quietly as I can, with the gun extended in front of me. When I'm close enough that I shouldn't miss if I have to shoot, I step quickly around the side of the chair and aim the gun.

It *is* Brad. His head is bowed, and it looks like he's fallen asleep sitting up.

"Brad?" I whisper loudly, praying he doesn't have the same hole in his forehead that Julie did.

He shivers, raises his head slowly, and then flinches with a startled half-cry. "Celine! How . . . why do you have a gun?"

"Damn. I'm sorry," I say quickly, lowering the gun to my side. "I took it from Hannah. She's dead or unconscious, I'm not sure which. But we have to hurry."

He pales suddenly. "Hannah's dead?" he whispers.

"Like I said, I don't know. That's why we have to hurry," I say. "Do you know where Alyssa is?"

Brad looks confused. "Alyssa?" he repeats.

"Yes. My daughter. *Your* daughter." I try not to get too frustrated with him. He's been kidnapped from the hospital, and he looks off, somehow. Maybe they drugged him. "Do you know where she is?"

"I . . . don't," he says slowly. "What about Jill?"

"She's definitely dead. Hannah shot her." I can't waste any more time with this. If he's not drugged, he has a head

181

injury or something. I'll have to get him on the way out. "Listen, I've got to find Alyssa," I say. "Just stay here. If you have a phone, call 911. I'll be back as soon as I can."

As I turn to leave, Brad's arm shoots out and his hand wraps around my wrist. There's surprising strength in his grip. "Are you *sure* Hannah's dead?" he says.

"No, I'm not!" I wrench away from him. "I'll be back soon, okay?"

I start away from the chair, toward the arched living room entrance. And that's when Hannah lurches into view—her hair matted and bloody, her smeared red lips pulled back from her clenched teeth.

"*Where is my daughter?*" I scream as I bring the gun up, fully intending to shoot her.

Something solid bumps my back, and a pair of strong arms wrap around me from behind, pinning my own arms to my sides.

Brad.

CHAPTER 32

"Let go of me!" I cry out, lunging futilely against the grip. "Brad, what the hell are you doing? Can't you see her? She's *right there!*"

The low, burbling laugh that comes from Hannah's throat chills my blood, and I stop moving.

"Oh, he can see me," she says, sauntering slowly toward me. She stops and plucks the gun easily from my straining fingers. "He's mine, Celine. He's *always* been mine."

I can't speak. I can't even breathe.

"Poor little Celine," Hannah drawls, laughing again. "You really thought he loved you, didn't you? That's my baby. I taught him how to sell it, and he delivered."

"Alyssa," I whisper. She's all I can think of now. "Please . . ."

"Don't beg me. It's disgusting," Hannah sneers. "None of this had to happen, you know. We were going to be together, filthy rich and happy, with all of my parents' money. All *he* had to do was break it off with you — but he chickened out." For an instant she glares past me at Brad. "And then he couldn't keep it in his pants, and managed to smash his stupid drunk ass into a concrete wall. But I went ahead with the plan. I killed them, and I waited. I knew he'd come back to me." Her smeared lips pull into a rictus of a smile. "And here he is."

"Hey. It's kind of a good thing I didn't keep it in my pants, isn't it?" Brad's voice rumbles through my back as he crushes me against him, keeping me from moving. "I mean, Jill did end up being useful."

"That's true," Hannah muses, striking a thoughtful pose. "I had no idea how crazy she was, how obsessed with Brad. But when I found out she'd killed Rosalie, I knew she'd fit in perfectly with my plans. So I recruited her." She tilts her head and smirks. "Staging a suicide had already worked out so well for me before, I thought I'd keep going."

Staged suicide . . . before Rosalie? "You mean Joan Carpenter," I rasp. "Don't you?"

"Of course I mean Joan. That stupid, simpering bitch." She snorts and rolls her eyes. "I knew you'd told Brad about her silly little website, so I pushed him to humiliate her. And he did — but she wouldn't take the hint. She was going to try twice as hard to land Brad. I had to kill her." Hannah gives me a sweet smile. "See, Celine, I've given you something to die with. Now you can let go of all that guilt over pushing poor little Joan to suicide. Jill told me how terrible you felt about it."

My anger is growing again, but I need to hold it for the right moment. If I'm going to get away from these two, I'll have to make it count the first time. "I thought Brad was all yours," I say with mocking concern. "Why would you have to worry about Joan going after him?"

Hannah shakes her head sympathetically. "I'll admit, she might have tempted Brad eventually," she says. "She *was* his type, and he can be quite the naughty boy on occasion. Sometimes he strays, and I have to punish him, but my man loves me." Her eyes narrow on her 'man.' "In fact, he's going to prove it right now by killing you."

"I am?" Brad says, but it's more surprise than reluctance.

"Yes, you are. Let go of her and take this." Hannah steps around me, wiggling the gun at him, and leans toward my ear. "Try to run, Celine, and I'll make him kill your daughter," she whispers. "I'd like to see you try and live with that."

I slump in place, demonstrating that I won't try to run.

Brad's arms fall away, and I stagger a few steps across the carpet. I won't turn to look at them. Hannah is a cold, horrible, lying deceitful creature who managed to fool me . . . but I'm about to return the favor. I only have to do it long enough to get out.

I hear the faint slap of flesh against metal as the gun exchanges hands. Despite everything that's happened, part of me still can't believe that Brad is going to kill me. Thinking about the truth of it makes my head ache.

After a moment, Brad says, "Do I *have* to shoot her? I've never killed anyone, you know. That's *your* job."

"Idiot!" There's a sharp sound that must be Hannah slapping him. "It's your job this time. Then we'll both be killers." I hear something slide and rustle, and Hannah whispers, "Murder is hot, baby. You have no idea how much it'll turn you on. Remember that time I came to your room, the night Joan died?"

Brad lets out a guttural moan, and thick bile surges up in my throat.

"Fine," he says. "But, Hannah . . . what if we get caught?"

"I swear to God, Brad! If you don't pull that trigger—"

As they argue, I tune them out slowly and shuffle away inch by inch, narrowing my focus to the living room entrance. All I have to do is run out, dash across the foyer and get through the front door. If I get a big enough head start, I can crawl through the hedges between this property and the Valentinos' house next door, which I sold them four years ago.

"—why you have to be such a baby! Just give it to me."

Go now.

I run.

Hannah lets out a scream of rage, just as I heave myself through the archway and pivot toward the door. A gunshot goes off behind me. I'm not hit, so I keep running, throwing a hand out to catch the door knob. The metal is cold as frost against my hot hand as I turn it and shove the front door open, crossing the porch in two leaps and diving down the steps.

I hit the ground, roll once and stand. I hear running footsteps pounding through the house.

And the wail of sirens closing in.

Oh God. Please be Ollie, I think desperately as I sprint down the front walk toward the street. Just as I shove through the gated iron fence separating the lawn from the curb, a squad car screams to a stop.

At the same time, a gun goes off from the house, and a patch of ground explodes a foot away from me.

Ollie is already out of the car, racing around the front. I wave my hands over my head. "She has a gun!" I scream.

There's another pop of gunfire, and I dive for the sidewalk. I feel the bullet pass over me. Answering fire thunders from the street, and I count at least four gunshots before loud silence settles over the world.

Something goes thud.

I pray it's Hannah.

CHAPTER 33

He got my message. I can't believe it. That was the worst attempt at a secret message in the history of secret messages, and Detective Oliver Chambers understood me.

Or maybe it was just one of his hunches.

I start to push off the ground, struggling to see who was shot. Then a strong hand wraps around mine and pulls me to my feet.

Ollie embraces me before I can take a breath.

"Didn't I tell you not to leave your house?" he says fiercely, but there's a trembling relief in his tone. "Jesus, Celine. I think I just killed Hannah Byers. What the hell's going on?"

I shudder and step back. "She was in on it. Her and Jill, they planned this together," I say. "And Brad. He's here, too. I think . . . oh, God. Alyssa!"

I'm sprinting back toward the house before he can react, but I hear his running footsteps hot on my heels. "Celine, wait! You just said someone else is here. Christ, will you let me go in first? I'm the one with the gun, here!"

I slow just enough to let him catch up with me. "Fine," I say through clenched teeth. "Just hurry."

"There'd better be a lot of explanation when this is over," he grumbles as he sprints ahead. "And you stay behind me, damn it."

Ollie reaches the wide-open front door and pauses for just a fraction of a second, gun upraised, before he swings through and points the weapon forward. "Police!" he booms. "Show yourself, and I won't shoot."

I'm only a few steps back. As much as I thought it wouldn't bother me, the sight of Hannah sprawled bloody and motionless on the steps has started my stomach churning again. But I catch up fast.

Ollie strides further into the house. "Police!" he yells again. "Is there anyone in here?"

A loud groan answers from the direction of the living room.

Ollie takes the time to glance sternly back at me. "Don't. Me first," he says.

I nod and follow on his heels. But when I'm able to see into the living room, I realize there's no need for concern. Brad is sitting on the floor, rocking back and forth, his bloody hands clamped across his equally bloody shin. "She shot me," he says through clenched teeth, looking up into the barrel of Ollie's gun. "That bitch *shot* me."

"Did she?" Ollie raises an eyebrow and glances at me.

I shake my head. "Not me. Hannah."

"Oh, God, what a mess." Ollie lifts a foot and plants it in the center of Brad's chest, shoving him to the floor. Brad lets out a squawk of protest. "Zip it. I don't know what *you* did, but you're under arrest."

Brad starts babbling as Ollie kneels next to him, holsters his gun, and flips him onto his stomach. "I didn't do anything!" he cries. "Look, you can't do this. I've been shot. I'm supposed to be in the hospital, you know. I'm the *victim* here! If you think—"

"I said, *shut up*." Ollie grinds a knee into the small of his back, pulls his wrists together and cuffs them neatly. "It's a flesh wound. You'll live."

"Ollie, I'm going," I say suddenly.

His head whips around, blue eyes blazing. "No, you're not."

"Alyssa is here somewhere, in this house," I tell him. "There's no one else here, at least not alive, and—"

"What do you mean, not alive?"

I sigh. "Jill's dead in the basement, and Julie's in the parlor. She was Hannah's live-in or something. She's dead too," I say. "And I'm *going* to find my daughter. The only way to stop me is to shoot me."

His eyes widen a fraction, and then he nods. "All right. If you're sure it's safe."

"I'm sure."

"Go, then." He pulls the radio from his belt. "I'm calling for backup."

I take a moment to smile at him. "Thank you."

"You're welcome."

With a quick nod, I sprint away and head up the stairs.

I've already searched the first floor, so she's got to be somewhere up here. Maybe Izzy is with her, wherever she is. But as awful as it seems, I'm not nearly as worried about Izzy as I am about my own daughter. She's my priority — now, always.

I check every bedroom, every closet and shower and bathtub, every hiding place big enough for a little girl. Nothing. Fear ripples through me as I climb the stairs to the stuffy attic and start searching around and under the furniture that's stored up here. She's *got* to be here.

If Hannah stashed her somewhere else, I might never get her back.

By the time I finish searching the attic and finding nothing, I'm furious all over again. I storm down the stairs, one flight and then the next, and run into the living room where Brad is sitting handcuffed in a chair, and Ollie is standing near the front window, watching for backup.

I grab Brad's shirt and wrench him forward. "Where is she?" I shout. "Tell me, or I'll blow a hole in your other leg, and then your third one!"

189

My outburst gets Ollie's attention. He comes over fast, his gun out and ready. "You can't find her?" he says quietly, with an edge of malice in his voice that's directed at Brad.

"No. She's not upstairs or in the attic, and I already searched the . . . first floor." Suddenly I remember the second kitchen, and the feature that would've been another selling point for the house if it actually worked. The dumbwaiter.

I let go of Brad and race toward the back of the house.

"Celine, wait!" Ollie shouts after me. "Would you stop *doing* that?"

"Be right back!" I call over my shoulder without stopping.

When I get to the second kitchen, I throw the light switch on and run to the dumbwaiter panel next to the cabinets. The Quintaines had it painted over, since it didn't work, but now the paint is scored away at the edges and scraped off the little knob that opens it. Hope surges in my heart as I twist the knob and throw the panel open.

She's there. My baby. Tied and gagged, tears streaking her dirty face. But alive.

"Alyssa!" I cry, working the gag from her mouth. She shivers and coughs, and I pick her up and carry her over to the kitchen counter. "Don't try to talk, baby. Mommy's here. I'm going to get these off you."

There's another tied and gagged little body in the dumbwaiter with her — Izzy. It looks like she's just unconscious, but I have to free Alyssa first.

"Ollie, come back here!" I shout as I hear more sirens arriving at the house. "Hurry. We might need an ambulance."

I yank three drawers open before I find a sharp knife, and quickly but gently cut through the ropes around my daughter's wrists and ankles. Her little body trembles, and when she's free, she wraps herself around me and buries her face in my neck.

"It's okay, munchkin. It's going to be okay," I soothe as I carry her back toward the dumbwaiter.

I'm trying to get Izzy out with one arm while I hold Alyssa with the other, when Ollie rushes in. He spots me, pushes me gently aside, and reaches in to scoop up the unconscious child.

Unconscious, but not dead. I can see the rise and fall of her chest.

"You don't have two daughters, do you?" Ollie says as he eases the gag out of the girl's mouth and carries her over to the counter, where the knife still lays.

I shake my head. "She's Hannah's daughter," I say. "Izzy."

"My best friend," Alyssa murmurs weakly on a shivering sob. "She's okay, isn't she?"

"Yes. She's going to be fine," I tell her as I rub her back and breathe in her scent. I'm not going to put her down for a long, long time. I may never let her out of my sight again.

I know that's not possible, but for now, it seems like the sanest plan in the world.

Ollie makes quick work of Izzy's bonds and holds her in his arms, easing her head up so she can breathe easier. "Come on," he says as he starts out of the kitchen. "I'm going to call an ambulance for her, but all three of you are getting in it."

"I'm fine. I don't need to go to the hospital."

"Really." He stops and nods at my arm. "You're bleeding, and there's a huge lump on the back of your head. You're going to the hospital."

I open my mouth to protest, but he gives me a look.

"Fine. I'm going," I say, my lips curving up slightly. "You're impossible, Detective Chambers. Do you know that?"

"*Me*? Which one of us snuck away from a police guard and confronted three people with guns, all by herself?"

"Jill didn't have a gun," I mutter. "She had a knife."

"My point still stands."

I guess I'll let him have this one. I'm too tired to argue, now that I don't have to fight anymore.

And I've got the whole world, right here in my arms.

CHAPTER 34

"Happy birthday, Alyssa!"

My daughter's excited squeal echoes through the house when Izzy shouts from the front door, and she slides off her chair and runs from the dining room. I laugh and follow her out, leaving the streamers I'd been trying to hang dangling from the chandelier.

The little girls collide in an explosion of giggles, jumping up and down a few times. Alyssa takes Izzy's hand and pulls her across the room, away from her foster parents, who are standing just behind her. "Come on, Izzy, I have a brand new yellow pony!" Alyssa gushes, still tugging her friend in the direction of her bedroom. "You can brush her, if you want to."

"Yes!" Izzy says enthusiastically.

I smile and shake my head as the girls vanish, and then turn to hug Missy Wilson — soon to be Missy Voltaire. "Thanks for coming early," I say. "Alyssa really wanted some alone time with Izzy before the rest of the guests get here."

"Oh boy. If we didn't come early, we'd never hear the end of it," Missy says with a laugh. "Right, Dan?"

Her fiancé nods behind the huge, wrapped present he's carrying. He's still a little shy, but get a drink or two in him and he loosens right up. Occasionally, if he has more than two drinks, he loosens *way* up.

Missy surprised me, and herself, by deciding to become a foster mother after she heard what happened with Hannah and Jill. We've talked almost daily since then. She had no idea how to be a mother, and Izzy is difficult to manage — not that it's her fault. She's already had enough trauma in her almost five years to last a lifetime. But Missy rose to the challenge.

She and Dan are planning to officially adopt Izzy once they're married.

"Are you actually going to bring them in, or are we all going to stand around in the living room staring at each other?"

I turn to Ollie and swat him playfully. He's the one who answered the door, but he'd backed away from the flurry of little girl glee when it started. Now he slips an arm around my shoulders and grins at Missy and Dan. "If she won't say it, I will," he says. "Come on in and have a seat, guys."

"Thank you," Missy says with a smile. "We'll do that."

The four of us head to the dining room. Dan places the present in the pile at the end of the table, and I step out to the kitchen, grabbing the pitcher of lemonade I'd made a few minutes ago and a stack of glasses. "So, how's the wedding prep coming?" I say.

"Fabulous. We're having Bel Votre cater the reception," Missy says, giving Dan's arm a light squeeze. "Oh, Celine, I almost forgot. Can you come with me sometime next week for a fitting? I can't *wait* until you see your bridesmaid's dress," she gushes.

"Sure. Just let me know when," I say with a smile that doesn't rise quite as high as it should. Bel Votre. The place Jill lied about going to when she went to see Brad, while they planned their horrific schemes.

Too much still reminds me of her, or Hannah, or Brad. I try not to let it bother me, but it's hard. I feel so betrayed — especially by Jill.

And she hurt Alyssa too. Badly. My bright, outgoing little girl is sometimes shy and quiet now, nervous around strangers.

She was too afraid to go to school for weeks after it was all over. She's easing back into it now, but it's still devastating to watch her struggle.

If Jill wasn't already dead, I'd have happily killed her. But both she and Hannah are in the ground, and Brad is locked away at the Seton-Frischer Clinic, the place where Hannah spent all those years. Unlike her, though, if he ever gets out of there, he'll go straight to jail for kidnapping, aiding and abetting, and attempted murder.

Ollie keeps close tabs on him. And I know that if Brad somehow escapes, he'll be dead before he ever gets near me.

"So, speaking of weddings," Missy says, leaning forward with a smile. "When are the two of you going to tie the knot?"

I laugh and glance at Ollie, who's wearing a funny crooked smile. "It's been less than a month," I tell her. "Give us a little more time before you try to ring the wedding bells. I don't even know what kind of toothpaste he uses yet."

"The kind that's on sale," he says with a grin. "I'm a cop. They don't pay us very much."

"Hey, what a coincidence," I say. "That's the kind I use, too."

"Well, then. I guess we're perfect for each other." He looks into my eyes, and a deep, pleasant shiver tugs at my gut. "We should get married."

I'm already thinking that someday soon, we will.

"Mommy!" Alyssa's small but enthusiastic shout precedes her as she races out of the bedroom, the yellow plastic pony she got last weekend clutched in one hand. Izzy is right behind her. "Mommy, can I give Izzy this one?" she says. "She doesn't have any yellow ones yet, only pink and blue, and I have two yellows."

I'm proud of my daughter for being so generous, and at the same time a little uneasy that she's so quick to give her brand new toys away. There's being kind, and then there's being generous to a fault. It's been so hard for me to stop doing the latter. I don't want my daughter to grow up a pushover like me and stay spineless until something horrible forces her to change.

But she's so earnest, and still so young. It probably won't hurt for now.

"Okay, munchkin. That's very sweet of you to share," I say.

Izzy cheers and nearly snatches the pony from my daughter's hand. "Thank you," she says quickly. It's almost an afterthought.

There's a gleam in the little girl's vivid blue eyes, so much like her mother's. She stares at Alyssa for just a moment too long and cocks her head — with the exact cold, calculating expression I saw on Hannah's face, seconds before she ordered Brad to kill me.

"Come on, 'Lyssa. Let's play some more ponies," Izzy says, and the moment vanishes as the girls giggle and tumble their way back to the bedroom.

But I wonder just how much of her mother is in Alice Isabel Byers . . . and how much of her father. Because now I know who that is: Brad Dowling.

The girls are sisters.

They don't know, and Missy and I have agreed not to tell them yet. The trauma of what happened at Hannah's house is still too fresh, and neither of them will really be able to understand what it means, that Brad is their father.

Maybe Izzy will turn out to have some of the same mental afflictions as her parents, or maybe not. A stable upbringing might help her overcome a lot of what had affected both Hannah and Brad — her a spoiled princess, him an idolized man-baby who was protected from everything. Maybe she'll be just fine, and the girls will stay best friends forever.

But I'm watching. Just in case.

And I'll always choose my daughter first.

THE END

THE JOFFE BOOKS STORY

We began in 2014 when Jasper agreed to publish his mum's much-rejected romance novel and it became a bestseller.

Since then we've grown into the largest independent publisher in the UK. We're extremely proud to publish some of the very best writers in the world, including Joy Ellis, Faith Martin, Caro Ramsay, Helen Forrester, Simon Brett and Robert Goddard. Everyone at Joffe Books loves reading and we never forget that it all begins with the magic of an author telling a story.

We are proud to publish talented first-time authors, as well as established writers whose books we love introducing to a new generation of readers.

We won Trade Publisher of the Year at the Independent Publishing Awards in 2023. We have been shortlisted for Independent Publisher of the Year at the British Book Awards for the last four years, and were shortlisted for the Diversity and Inclusivity Award at the 2022 Independent Publishing Awards. In 2023 we were shortlisted for Publisher of the Year at the RNA Industry Awards.

We built this company with your help, and we love to hear from you, so please email us about absolutely anything bookish at feedback@joffebooks.com

If you want to receive free books every Friday and hear about all our new releases, join our mailing list: www.joffebooks.com/contact

And when you tell your friends about us, just remember: it's pronounced Joffe as in coffee or toffee!

ALSO BY SONYA BATEMAN

STANDALONES
HE CAME BACK FOR MY DAUGHTER
THE HUSBAND KILLER
THE REALTOR

Made in United States
North Haven, CT
10 May 2024

52312650R00125